Some New Ambush

CARYS DAVIES won second prize in the inaugural 2002 Orange Harpers&Queen Short Story Competition, second prize in the 2005 Asham Award, and runner-up prizes in the 2005 Bridport Prize and the 2006 Fish Short Histories Prize. Her stories have appeared in prize anthologies, in *The London Magazine,* and in a variety of U.S. literary magazines, including *New Letters, Kestrel* and *G.W. Review.* *Some New Ambush* is her first story collection.

Some New Ambush

Carys Davies

CAMBRIDGE

PUBLISHED BY SALT PUBLISHING
Acre House, 11–15 William Road, London NW1 3ER, United Kingdom

First published 2007
Reprinted 2011

Printed and bound in the United Kingdom by Lightning Source
Typeset in Swift 9.5/13

ISBN 978 1 84471 341 7 paperback

1 3 5 7 9 8 6 4 2

For Michael

Contents

Hwang

For the past three-quarters of an hour, I have been sitting here in the coffee shop of the Barnes & Noble bookstore on Diversey Avenue with Ellen, as I do every Tuesday morning between ten forty-five and eleven thirty. Inevitably, we have been talking about Hwang.

I first met Hwang on a Monday afternoon five years ago, the spring Francis and I arrived here from Cleveland. He was living then, as he does now, with his old mother and his beautiful daughter in a tiny apartment on the corner of Diversey and Clark, a short distance from our house.

He is a small, lean man of indeterminate age. He could be forty, he could be sixty, I don't know. Every day he is dressed the same: the same pair of black felt carpet slippers, the same loose wool trousers suspended from a crumbling leather belt, the same threadbare khaki shirt with short limp sleeves and one breast pocket. He never smiles. His fingers are scaly and curled like a cockerel's toes, he has the quick, searching neck of a lizard, the watchful face of a cruel emperor, a ruthless bandit; the face of a person you might go to for the execution of some stealthy but vicious crime.

Hwang is my dry cleaner—mine and Ellen's—and I have been going to him now for the best part of five years, usually twice a week. Once on a Monday afternoon to drop off Francis's shirts, once on a Friday morning to collect them. Other items—Francis's suits and ties, my blouses, dresses and skirts—I usually take in with the shirts unless there's some emergency on another day, something that's been forgotten or that needs doing in a hurry. In which case I make a special trip in the middle of the week, maybe two. Mostly, I would say, I am at Hwang's at least three times a week.

A few people in the neighborhood prefer not to use him. They think he is scary and rude, which is true. He is probably the most frightening and offensive person I have ever met.

Generally you go in, your arms laden with the week's cleaning, and stand there for a full two minutes while he ignores you, his face wearing its permanent mask of furious scorn, carrying on as if you weren't there, shuffling back and forth in his tattered carpet slippers, sorting piles of laundry on the counter, throwing shirts into the giant wheeled hamper behind, dry cleaning items into a mountain on the floor; other items needing repair he hurls in the direction of his ancient mother, who sits in the corner, dressed entirely in gray, crouched over a dressmaker's sewing machine and an enormous rack of at least a hundred spools of different colored thread.

When he is ready, you are allowed to put your dirty laundry on the counter. His system is no different from any other dry cleaner in the neighborhood, no different from any other dry cleaner anywhere, really: one ticket for you, a copy for him to keep with your laundry to identify it when it is ready to collect. Hwang's tickets are pink and he keeps a pad of them on the counter, next to a dish of wrapped boiled sweets which I think he puts there for the children—though, as Ellen says, show me the child that would dare reach up under Hwang's assassin's glare and take one!

When he has checked your things into the appropriate piles, he fills out your pink tickets (separate ones for laundry and dry cleaning) in his jagged scrawl, tears each one from the pad with a sharp, brutal twist of his bony wrist, and thrusts them in your face. In my case he usually barks *Flyday* at this point.

When I return on Fridays for Francis's shirts, or in the middle of the week for any other oddments that are ready, I hand Hwang my pink ticket, or tickets if I have more than one, and he shuffles off into the back, muttering and truculent, under the racks and racks of cellophane-wrapped garments, each one labeled with one of his duplicate tickets. When he has located your things, he brings them to you without a smile, and impales your old ticket on the sharp spike he keeps next the bowl of boiled sweets. I have often pictured him, as he does this, in the stony yard of some village, wringing the necks on a row of shabby chickens, though I have come to realize I might be wrong about that.

The worst thing about Hwang —much worse than the not-smiling and the grumpy shuffling about in the felt slippers—the thing that most appalls people, the thing that frightens some of them away completely, is what happens if you lose the pink ticket he has given you.

'No Ticky,' he says then with vicious finality and something like triumph. 'No Shirty.' Clamps his little mouth shut, folds his ropy arms across his limp khaki shirt, and glares at you. A proud, challenging, disdainful glare it is impossible to ignore.

It has happened to me before now, and it has happened to Ellen. In fact when it happened to Ellen, a couple of years back, Hwang practically reduced her to tears. He stood there repeating that hideous rhyming couplet of his while she balanced her purse on her knee and hunted through it for her ticket, which wasn't there. When she begged him to try and find her things without the help of a numbered ticket Hwang just stabbed the air with his cockerel's claw, indicating the row upon row upon row of garments hanging from the ceiling awaiting collection, as if inviting Ellen to dream up a more impossible task. Eventually, that time, he did give way, puffing and sighing and making a huge fuss of rustling all the clothes in their cellophane covers as he looked through.

These days, he is less obliging. He has become much worse about this business of the tickets.

What brings people back to Hwang in spite of his rudeness, is that he is cheap—at 99 cents a shirt he is cheaper than anyone else in the neighborhood—and his work is excellent. Also his old mother, sitting wordlessly all day in her little corner, carries out repairs and alterations of the highest quality; invisible mends like healed skin.

And then there is Moon.

Hwang's beautiful daughter.

It is worth going to Hwang's just to gaze for a few minutes at Moon. She is now, I would say, about sixteen years old. She has a broad, exquisite face, hair the color of a raven's wing, cut to her chin. I've said to Ellen many times that if Francis and I were ever to change places, if I were to go downtown every morning and spend the day behind his gleaming desk at First Boston and he were to collect his shirts from Hwang's on a Friday afternoon when Moon was in there doing her schoolwork, he would never come home again.

Moon wears the navy and forest green uniform of one of the private Catholic schools in the city: pleated plaid skirt, green wool blazer, white blouse with a piped Peter Pan collar which always looks as if it has been starched and pressed that very morning by Hwang himself.

There are a handful of such schools in the city, where the discipline is strict, the education narrow but reliable, where uniforms are worn and the fees are relatively modest. Still, you can see what a struggle it is for Hwang. How he glares at that laundry hamper with its 99 cent shirts inside. Hwang looks as though he will die in his slippers paying those fees so that Moon won't have to run the shop after he's gone.

We have been talking about Hwang and Moon, this morning, Ellen and I.

We have both noticed them lately, arguing in the shop. Moon looking sullen and rebellious and not sitting down at the table in the corner next to her grandmother where she is supposed to do her homework. Hwang pointing a curled finger at her books and making himself look even uglier than usual with all this shouting at Moon. Looking as if he is telling his daughter that he hasn't crammed his soul into his threadbare khaki shirt, his crumbling leather belt, so that she can grow up to become a dry cleaner. One terrible scene I witnessed ended with Hwang throwing the bowl of boiled sweets up into the air, along with a whole pile of pink tickets snatched up off the spike on the counter. The sweets bounced across the floor and out across the sidewalk into the gutter, the tickets floated about in the steamy shop like butterflies and even the old woman looked up for a moment from her work in the corner to see what was going on. Then Moon ran off in tears through the curtain in the back, up into the tiny apartment above.

Ellen and I discuss Hwang's ambitions for his daughter, and end up agreeing that with her grave, exquisite face, her raven-wing hair, she looks so much like a fairy-tale princess that ambition and hard work may not matter for her, because *some one* is surely bound to come along one day, and whisk her away from the chemical smells and the drone of her grandmother's sewing machine and the damp kiss and sigh of her father's steam press.

Ellen is my friend.

She has been my friend ever since the day Francis and I arrived here five years ago, ever since the spring afternoon she came across the street from her house to ours, bearing a tray of iced-tea and three white saucers of Pepperidge Farm cheddar cheese Goldfish, one saucer for each of us. She has lived all her life in the neighborhood, grew up here and lived here with her husband Norm until he died of cancer nine years ago. The day after we moved in, she came back over and took my arm and walked me around our little area here, where I have come to feel so much at home: the small but adequate A&P; the two good hairdressers; our dentist, Dr. Sandusky. The Barnes & Noble bookstore with its coffee shop, where I have coffee with Ellen every Tuesday morning, where I am having coffee with her at this very moment. The Ann Sather café where Francis and I go for a pancake breakfast on Saturdays. There is the Swedish butcher; a chiropodist; a medium-sized Walgreens; four small but thriving theaters the three of us attend whenever there is something showing which appeals. The hospital and medical center are only four blocks from our house. There is Hwang too of course, less than three minutes' walk away, and the branch library where I attend a book group every third Wednesday in the month and Ellen comes across to cook Francis his supper and keep him company.

Francis has promised me we will never have to move again; we've moved so much over the years with First Boston, and I have found that as I've grown older, settling into a new place is something I do increasingly badly. I did it worse in Cleveland than in Atlanta, worse in Atlanta than in Philadelphia and everywhere worse since the children left.

It has been different here. I have found I have everything I want; all my needs seem to be looked after in this half square mile with all its now familiar places. I have Francis, and I have Ellen, and I have always felt that there is nothing else here I could possibly ask for.

Much of my conversation with Ellen revolves, inevitably, around the neighborhood. Speculation about whether the new extension to the Ann Sather café will be ready by the end of the summer. How much longer it takes to find what you want in the A&P since they changed everything around. I tell Ellen which book has been chosen for the next meeting of my Wednesday library group and from time to time I try to persuade her to come along with me, at which she laughs and throws up her hands so her silver bangles slip and clatter along her arms, and says, 'What! And have Francis starve?'

We wonder about the funny smell from the roadworks at the intersection of Clark and Lincoln where they have dug up part of the sidewalk in front of the dental surgery, about how the new young man with the red hair at the Swedish butcher's might have lost his thumb; and at some point on these Tuesday mornings, sooner or later, we end up talking about Hwang or his old mother or Moon.

The other week I said to Ellen that Hwang reminded me, with his baggy wool pants and his ruthless lack of mercy, of a ninja. A ninja about to pounce.

Ellen hooted at this, threw up her hands. Her silver bangles clanked. 'A *ninja!* Hardly, Sal! Ninjas are *Japanese.* You can't think Hwang is *Japanese!*'

Ellen was almost choking with laughter, fanning her hand in front of her mouth so her bangles started clanking again.

'*Korean.* He's from *Korea.* All the dry cleaners here are Korean now.'

She said that when her mother was a girl here they were all Jewish owned; now it's the Koreans; one day, she said, it will be another lot.

Ellen was a schoolteacher once and very occasionally she can still sound a little like one; she can sound ever so slightly lecturing.

'No,' she repeated, still chuckling, '*not* Japanese.'

I shrugged. 'I know that, Ellen.'

For a moment we were silent, Ellen took a bite out of whatever kind of cookie she was having that day, a sip of coffee.

'He still makes me think of a ninja,' I said.

In fact, I had always thought Hwang was from China. Or rather, I'd never really thought much about exactly where he was from. I'd wondered why he is the way he is, so bitter and angry and haughty. I'd wondered if there was a Mrs. Hwang, if perhaps she had been too frightened to come here with him and start a new life in America, if she might still be over there somewhere, if Hwang was still trying to send for her. I'd wondered, also, if he had perhaps once occupied some position of rank, if that accounted for his brutal disdain, his bullying rudeness, the impression he gives of so much swallowed pride. Of bitterness, maybe, at the way life has betrayed him, or been so hard.

Perhaps his difficulties with Moon are getting him down. I don't know.

What is certain is that over the years that I've known him he has grown angrier, more frightening, meaner to his ticketless patrons. Where once he would eventually shuffle off, with a lot of bad-tempered mumbling, to search through all the hanging clothes for the items in question, these days he will not budge. He just stands there behind the counter, shaking his head and looking mean; obdurate as a stone.

I have always liked Barnes & Noble for coffee. The green paint and brown wood are soothing, the plush carpet is soft underfoot, there is an atmosphere of quiet repose, and the cakes are good. Today I am having a tall latte and a slice of cherry crumb cake, Ellen a lemon cookie and a decaff espresso.

She is wearing a fawn linen pantsuit and a cream cotton blouse cut square across her collarbones. A print scarf around her throat—she doesn't like her throat, she says no one our age should go out with her throat uncovered. She looks well-groomed, rested, at peace. She looks exactly like herself.

It is six days since I came back from the library and found one of Ellen's silver bangles in our bed and I can think of no sensible way to proceed. I am frightened of speaking, of saying a single word, either to Ellen, or to Francis. I'm certain that if I put anything of what I feel into words, I will poison the air we breathe and none of us will ever recover. I have become increasingly certain over the past week that the best thing to do is to say nothing, to let things run their course. To stay quiet until whatever is going on has come to a close; to hope for some kind of invisible mend.

When we are almost ready to leave, Ellen says she won't be a second, she just needs to go to the bathroom. I watch her get up, thread her way between the little round tables. At the first bookcase she turns, points back at her chair, mouths, Watch my purse a second?

Ellen's Cole Haan purse, boxy and black with two tall handles, is sitting upright on her chair. The shiny leather is cool to the touch. The zipper makes almost no sound. There is very little inside. House-keys. A hairbrush. Chase Manhattan checkbook in a navy blue plastic case, a single lipstick, her maroon wallet. I fan my thumb across the checkbook stubs looking for I don't know what. The lipstick is nearly finished, its scent powdery and delicious, the scent of Ellen herself. In her wallet she has forty-five dollars and some loose change. A receipt from the One-Hour Photo on Clark Avenue, a pink dry-cleaning ticket.

There is one last mouthful of cherry crumb cake left on my plate. I pick it up with my fingertips, put it in my mouth. Then I eat the dry-cleaning ticket.

It is, I know, a small, stupid thing to do.

I know also that I might just as well have crushed it in my palm and dropped it into the metallic trash can over by the cakes, or just slipped it into my jacket pocket—it's very unlikely Ellen would ever have found it in either place. But sitting here now, thinking of Ellen's silver bangle, the shock of it against my foot, eating the ticket seems the only available thing to do. It is almost impossible to chew, it skates between my upper and lower teeth like the squeaky scraps of articulating paper Dr. Sandusky has me bite on when he's checking a crown or a new filling. In the end I munch it into a ball and with one painful swallow it's gone and all that's left in my mouth is the sharp, inky taste of Hwang's bitter scrawl. A picture in my mind of Ellen, rooting hopelessly through her purse. Hwang behind the counter, arms folded. His pugnacious fury, his proud, frigid grandeur. Fixing her with his ninja's glare.

Waking the Princess

She was the widow of the Customs House clerk and she had never liked me. I was only after one thing, she said, and I could forget about that because I repulsed her. I *disgusted* her. She loathed the sight of me and as long as I lived, she told me, I would *never ever* find the key to her heart.

I had tried to kiss her once outside her front door—a terrible, greedy, darting, desperate sort of lunge I have always regretted—and after that she took to shouting at me through the window when I came to call.

'Lizard!' she shouted. 'Toad!'

Her name was Elizabeth and she lived with her children in one of the tiny dark houses which lined the narrow streets behind the Customs House in our town at that time. Every day she appeared at her door in the same dingy, high-necked gown, her brown hair scraped back and pinned behind, a drawn look to her face. But she was tall and strong and big-boned and to me she resembled the gorgeous painted figureheads on the ships that came up the river and lay anchored outside the warehouses on the quay. I thought about her all the time.

I had brought her presents—a paper flower from the fair at Appleby, a tea canister with a design of roses on it from Atkinson's on China Street, a pair of combs for her hair—but she left everything on the doorstep for the beggars to steal. I sent her letters and poems but she screwed them up in her fist and tossed them out into the sewers; when I called she closed the door in my face and shouted at me through the window and I was left to loiter in the street outside her house with nothing to do but wait and watch for a glimpse of her.

Which was how I began to observe the way she lived.

The front door was almost always open and I could see the dead clerk's shabby black coat, still hanging on its hook in the passageway. I could see her ragged children running in and out all day long. Elizabeth herself seemed to do nothing but tend the fire and clean the floor. In the early mornings, she was there crouched in the crooked doorway, a donkey-stone in her hand, whitening the edge of the step. The rest of the time I could see her through the open door, trudging around with a bucket of water, a handful of brushes and a heap of rags. Half her life, she seemed to spend on the floor, trying to scrub it clean—all the time with her dirty children charging in from the street, down the dismal passageway beyond the front door, mud and sewer-slop dropping off the flaking soles of their boots and mingling with the blown soot from the fire and sinking into the furrowed boards and lumpy flagstones of the floor. She'd yell at them then to look at the stinking grime they'd brought in on their shoes from the filthy street and how they were trampling it into the floor.

Once a month she bought clean sand from the old man who hauled it into town from the shore on his cart. Then she'd be on her knees again, scouring her pock-marked flags and greasy, blackened floorboards with the sand and a bucket of steaming water. As far as I could tell, she owned just one carpet, a small woven thing like a tab-rug only heavy. This she would heave out into the street every Monday morning on her back, like a stevedore, then beat it against the stone wall of the house. Vast puffs of black dust drifted up into the air, getting smaller and gradually paler until she seemed to be satisfied, and then she'd drag the carpet back into the mean, dark little room at the front of the house she called *the parlour*. She only seemed to rest for a few hours a week, on Sunday morning, when she'd stand at her bedroom window wrapped up in a blanket. There she would shake out her drab, solitary dress and beat it like her old carpet until it was as clean as it ever would be, and then she'd put it on again and go to church.

I decided I wouldn't bother any more with the tea canisters, the paper flowers, the combs for her hair, the poetry. I would give her something she would value above anything. I would give her something that would change her life.

I visited shops and markets and fairs. I looked in newspapers and catalogues and scrounged enough money to travel the country. I went to Manchester and Edinburgh and to the Great Exhibition at the Crystal Palace but found nothing anywhere that came close to what I had in mind.

I decided I would make what I wanted myself.

Something different. Something new.

I did more research; I investigated the price of raw materials. At the end of nine months I bought what I could afford, the rest I stole late at night from the warehouses along the quayside. In the end, after weeks of skulking around and waiting, I bought or stole everything I needed—china clay from Fowey in Cornwall, linseed oil from the Baltic, cork from Morocco. After half a winter hanging about at the docks in Liverpool I got rosin; in Glasgow, naptha and jute.

In my room I ground the cork with the pestle from my landlady's kitchen and mixed everything in a bucket to a nice gloopy kivver. I hung the jute on a tall wood frame. I dragged a ladder upstairs and troweled my secret recipe onto the jute. When that was dry, I smoothed and polished it with pumice. I worked night and day. I mixed a varnish and tested its consistency on my tongue, and once that was on, and dry, I was ready. I shaved in hot water and dressed in a clean shirt. With a sharp meat knife I cut a small section away from the frame, rolled it inside a piece of brown paper, and with my heart knocking in my chest like a hammer, set off with it under my arm.

It was late in the evening when I arrived. I had not called at her house in nearly a year. She had lost weight. The skin of her beautiful face looked grey, almost transparent with fatigue. In one hand she carried a stiff broom, in the other, a damp foul-smelling rag. She sighed.

'You,' she said, weary, impatient, and began to close the door, but this time I was too quick for her. I got my shoe into the space next to the crooked door-frame and began to peel the brown paper away from the package. In the quiet street, in the darkness, the paper crackled, and beneath it the stuff shone with a light of its own.

'Look, Elizabeth,' I said. 'I have brought you something.'

In the pale light coming from her house, the weird cloth glowed. It gleamed like the belly of a fish. She reached out and she touched it.

'What is it?' she said.

I took off the rest of the brown paper and bent to the gutter for a handful of muck. 'Look,' I said, and smeared it across the silken surface of the cloth, then took the rag from her fingers and in one swift easy movement, wiped it clean again.

She gasped, and let me in.

In the parlour I laid the cloth on the splintered floor, scooped a handful of soot and ash up out of the hearth and scattered the whole lot over the cloth.

This time she clapped. Two quick hurried smacks, one hand against the other.

'The rag!' she said. 'Quickly!'

She was laughing now. I'd never seen her look so happy. In fact I realised now I'd never seen her look happy at all ever. She'd become almost playful, as if in bringing her something that would change her life I had also introduced her to an exciting and delicious new game.

'The rag!'

In my haste to get into the house I had dropped her rag outside in the gutter. Both of us scanned the room now, hunting for something to use to wipe away the smuts. I had nothing with me—no necktie, no handkerchief, nothing. I waited for Elizabeth to run to the kitchen for something, but she seemed irritated, exasperated at the delay—too excited and eager to bother going to fetch anything. She looked down at her dress and lifted the hem. For a moment she held it between her fingers and seemed about to use it on the smuts, but then she seemed to remember that the dingy garment was the only one she possessed; that it was too precious to use. She let it fall, and began instead to loosen her hair, pulling out the pins which held it in a neat mound above the buttoned collar at the back of her dress. Then she sank to her knees and as she wiped away the scattered soot and ash with her hair, her face seemed to glow with delight. She knelt there, gazing at the precious cloth, fascinated.

Then—and I had not expected this—she began to unbutton her boots and when they were off, she removed her stockings. Long grey knitted things that had covered her legs like chain mail.

I watched as her feet came into view for the first time. Pale and perfect and very white against the black of her skirt and the gloom of the horrid little parlour—nothing like her poor calloused hands which were rough and criss-crossed like an old fisherman's with deep lines and scars. She stood on the cloth and arched her back.

'Aah,' she sighed and closed her eyes and I knew that in her whole life she had never felt such a cool kind of smoothness beneath her feet, such a clean softness. I pictured all her children racing barefoot along pristine passageways, stepping pink and scrubbed out of a warm tub onto my satin-finished floors.

'Does it have a name, Henry?' she said, her voice soft and dreamy and contented.

'Does it?'

Henry. She had never called me Henry before. Always *Toad* or *Lizard* or some other unpleasant and insulting thing.

Upstairs one of her children had begun to moan in its sleep but she didn't seem to notice. She was too busy flexing her bare toes on the cloth.

'Well?'

I had thought long and hard about a name for my creation and it had come to me in the end in a kind of day-dream one evening while I sat slumped on the floor in the corner of my room, exhausted after working so hard for so long, waiting for the stuff to dry. I had been sitting for hours, breathing in the mellow fragrance of the linseed, and a name—smooth as the cloth itself—had drifted into my mind.

I repeated it now. She mouthed the word slowly, stumbling over the syllables as if I had given her a tongue-twister, mixing up the *l*s and the *n* and making both of us laugh, until at last she got it right. She was smiling—a dizzy, ecstatic, faraway smile—dreaming like me I am sure of how the linoleum would cast its lustrous moonshine over all the rooms of her little house and drive out the forces of darkness that haunted every grimy corner, every broken floorboard, every pitted, potholed flagstone, and I have always, always wished that at that moment I could somehow have managed to do things differently. I have always wished I could somehow have managed to take everything just a little more slowly. But I lunged forward then, burying my face in her hair and covering her neck with dry, hungry kisses. 'Elizabeth,' I groaned and pulled her close. One of my knees began to pry its way between her sturdy legs. My fingers fumbled with the tiny buttons at her throat.

With the force of a falling tree branch she slapped away my hand.

'Snake,' she hissed in my ear, and stepped off the linoleum.

Her eyes flashed and her smile was gone and she was straightening the rumpled collar of her dress; she was pulling on her chain mail stockings and shaking the soot from her hair and pinning it up more quickly than I would have thought possible.

'Goat,' she said, in a hard, quiet voice and pushed the precious cloth across the floor towards me with the edge of her toe.

'I'm sorry Elizabeth,' I said, humbly, but she ignored me and carried on straightening her clothes as if I had not spoken.

Last of all there was the brisk popping sound of her buttoning her boots, and then she looked at me and shook her head and laughed a little and said, how could I ever have thought she would be that easy?

Monday Diary

My name is Flipper Harries and I am a gift from God.

Neither the midwife nor Dr. Beynon was ready to catch me when I came shooting out like a sleek fish into the hot little room. Through the open door, my sister, Tanya, stared at the creature lying in the kicked-up sheets of our mother's bed. Green and glistening with a small red face and at its shoulders—Tanya could see—tiny wings, coiled like the ferns on the mountain behind town in springtime.

Tanya was sent to give the news to our father. She searched through all the dark legs in the Red Cow, but his big shape was lost somewhere in the warm noisy crowd along the bar. The only face she knew belonged to Voyle Peg, alone in a shadowy corner, sprinkling salt on his crisps, the dark blue skin of his face glowing beneath the fluorescent lights. He saw her too and knew that I'd arrived.

'Boy or girl then, Tanya?' he asked my four year old sister, cupping his hand behind his ear and stooping closer to her face for the answer.

Tanya, very serious, shook her head.

'Neither.'

And then, in a whisper so small he could barely hear it, 'An angel.'

She spotted dad then and went running off to tell him the good news and Voyle Peg was left opening and closing his thin navy lips without making a sound.

When my mother wouldn't look at me, dad sent for the minister, Mr. Morgan, because he didn't know what else to do.

Mr. Morgan took me, wrapped like a pupa, like an ordinary baby, from the midwife. 'Remember, Marion,' he said to my mother, 'every baby is a gift from God.'

When she didn't move, he put me on the pillow next to her face. 'This one is too.'

None of them knew yet that the doctor's magic pills were to blame for the way I am. (He'd fed them months ago to my sick mother with a cool glass of water and she'd called him *a miracle worker*). Nobody knew then, not even Dr. Beynon, that there were other babies being born all over just like me, hands like wings and no arms at all.

My mother has kept those words of Mr. Morgan's, like something precious in a box. She has a way of seeing inside me, and at certain moments during the day, she comes over and takes my face in her hands and looks into my eyes and repeats them to me. 'Remember, David, you are a gift from God.'

My name is Flipper Harries and I am fifteen years old.

I'm surprisingly good at rugby, terrible at the piano. At school I'm considered neither stupid nor clever. I'm cleverer than Mr. Clark thinks—he's forever yelling over the noise, 'No shouting out. Hands up!' But he doesn't mean *hands up*, he means *arms up*, and in the forest of limbs he never notices my waggling hand, flapping like a flannel with the answer.

I'm cleverer than Tom Ellis, and quite often, I do his school-work for him. I've perfected his handwriting, the tall left-sloping *t*s and the way his *u*s are almost closed at the top like an *a*. I've been doing it, off and on, for ten years, ever since we were in class one and did Monday morning diaries. He could never think of anything to put, so I began taking things out of my life and writing them into his:

On Saturday we went all the way to Porthcawl for Angela Hansford's birthday. Flipper bought her a pet chicken for a present. Her dad has built a wooden hut for it in the back yard.

A gypsy read Flipper's fortune with a pack of greasy cards. He wouldn't tell anyone what she said.

Tom Ellis is probably the most beautiful boy who has ever lived.

He has dark hair and dark skin and a narrow jaw and such a serious, almost stony expression that when he smiles it feels like a prize you have won.

He's tall and lean and there's not one single girl in the entire valley who's not in love with him. His mother accentuates his beauty with the clothes she gives him to wear, most of which she makes herself. She knits strange, striped shirts for him and washes them in Dreft so they always have a sweet fresh smell in them which I've come to think of as *his* smell. All of them are soft and fall in folds from his shoulders like the loose wrapping on a present. When the girls get half a chance, they stroke and tug at his shirts.

It's a mystery how anyone as fat and ugly as Annie Ellis could have produced some one like Tom. There's something strange and foreign in his looks, his skin has a dry, dusty quality quite unlike the soft pale skin of the people here. He's like a warm thing that's fallen out of the sky into our damp little town. It's impossible to think of him ever going underground and turning pale like the men here, and old before his time. I think that's partly what the girls love about him, that he's different, that he doesn't seem to belong here. He's like the bright vinyl paint the girls' mothers put on their doors and window frames, Tango and Bermuda Blue, a bit of colour and excitement against the dark stone of the houses and the black of the mountain and the mine. He's all the colour and excitement of their lives. When he and I are together, they follow us about like a plume of smoke, all watching and waiting to see who he'll chose.

On Wednesday evenings, I walk down the hill and slip inside the Co-op. If I've got some money I buy something, otherwise I pretend to be looking at the pyramids of John West salmon. I hang about as long as I dare, wanting to stay but also wanting to clear off before my loitering gets on Minty Clegg's nerves—before she looks up from filing her dirty nails and mutters, 'Fuck off, Flipper.'

Minty Clegg works in the Co-op on Wednesdays after school with Angela Hansford. They both serve behind the counter and wear green nylon shopcoats.

Minty Clegg is a stale-looking girl with sparse hair, and large, sharp teeth. She wears her shop coat very short and has rough,blotchy legs. When Tom comes in she smiles, baring her sharp teeth and a pulse flickers in the hollow of her freckled throat above the cold zip of her shopcoat.

Angela stays where she is behind the counter, watching too. She is quite small with short brown hair and I have been in love with her my whole entire life. I think if I could eliminate this one fact from my life, I could be happy.

She lives three doors down from us. If I lean out of my parents' window upstairs I can see the smoke from the Hansfords' fire chugging out of the chimney. I can see a sliver of Angela's bedroom window and sometimes a corner of her blue curtains blowing against the sill. The chicken I gave her for her fifth birthday died years ago but the wooden hut her dad built is still there in the yard. Tom has never told me what he thinks of her and I've never asked him.

All I can think of is that he will chose her. These past months, I can feel how she's begun to creep between me and Tom, something that rubs against us, like a tiny seed of tragedy.

In the bottom drawer of the pine chest in my bedroom, underneath a pillowcase, I have hidden a set of Tom Ellis's clothes. One of his knitted long-sleeved shirts and a pair of his soft homemade trousers. They still have his sweet fresh smell in them. They are neatly folded and ready to put on.

For some time now I've been avoiding my mother because of her trick of looking inside me. She's been looking at me in quiet moments of the day when dad is asleep and Tanya is out.

When she thinks I've been sitting too long without saying anything, she comes up to me and touches my cheek with the back of her hand.

I never planned to steal the clothes, and, really, it's not that I've stolen them, it's that he gave them to me and I've not given them back. A little while ago it was so hot one day after school that we went swimming in the black pond in the Dip at the bottom of town with all our clothes on. We had a bath at Tom's house and he gave me a set of his clothes to wear.

I don't know if it was in my mind then to keep them, but I do know that when I put them on I didn't feel like Flipper Harries any more.

Yesterday I left a note in Angela's desk. I didn't sign it but I wrote it in Tom's handwriting, the same writing I use when I do his schoolwork for him, with the tall *t*s and the round *u*s. *I will be under the trees by the stream in the Dip tomorrow at nine o'clock. Please come.*

Undressing, I glimpse myself in the long wardrobe mirror, stooping over the clothes. It's such a shock to see my old familiar body that I close my eyes against the sight of it and pull the knitted shirt over my head, but a cold skin has begun to close around my heart and before I know it the thought of Voyle Peg's plastic leg is bringing a swelling into my throat, because even though Voyle is old and dying from the coal dust silted up in his yellow lungs, he can still stand on the pavement outside the Red Cow with the creases of his trousers breaking over his black shoes and no one would ever know there was a plastic leg hiding inside. He can go about with his peg between his shoe and his bum and if you didn't know, you'd be completely fooled.

But this feels to me like the only chance I'll ever have. In ten minutes she'll be there, searching in the dark for the bright white gleam of the stripes in Tom Ellis's long-sleeved shirt.

'David?' calls my mother from the front room.

I do tell her goodbye but I'm not sure if she hears. My voice comes out as a croak, and then I'm out the door into the night, the cuffs of his shirt tucked carefully into my belt.

It's so quiet here tonight, nothing but the shuffle of branches above my head, a slow dropping where the water slides into the black pond.

Here she comes.

A little way from me still, she stops, and seems to give her head a little shake. In the dark I can't see her face, only the shimmer of her blouse. One of the empty sleeves has worked loose from my belt and in the cool breeze I can feel it wafting about, like a scarf.

For a long frozen moment I stand with my eyes closed and pray for the thick waters of the black pond to rise up and swallow me whole.

'You're a daft idiot,' she whispers, and laughs quietly into the darkness. There's a soft cracking in the long grass beneath her feet, the cold touch of her hands under the woollen cloth of the perfumed shirt. She reaches up under the shirt and holds my face between her hands and kisses me on the mouth. Still holding my face, Angela Hansford pulls me down into the grass.

Oh bloody hell. Oh Jesus *Christ*!

MY NAME IS FLIPPER HARRIES AND I AM GIFT FROM GOD!!!!!!!!!!!!

Gingerbread Boy

I always hoped it wasn't someone old who took Bobby. He was afraid of old people. He'd look at the yellow whites of their eyes and their ugly teeth and the shiny brown skin on their hands and then he'd push his face into Lily's skirts and hide. He was afraid of old people and dogs and witches, though he was very fond indeed of fairy tales and I always thought it likely that he was lured away, not with the offer of sweets or a drive in a nice car, but with the promise of a story. He was like Lily that way—you have to hold onto Lily when you come out of the cinema so she doesn't fall under a pram or a bus. You have to hold onto her until she comes back to herself, until you're sure she's not still dreaming about the fading characters in the film.

We should have called the police immediately of course, but when you open the back door and you can't see your four-year-old where he was five minutes ago, playing on the flagstones with his blue metal car, you don't think, 'He's gone. Someone has taken him and he's gone.' You experience a little jolt, yes, your face goes hot, there's the icy, shrinking feeling in your chest you get whenever they give you some kind of scare, but you don't think, 'This is it. This is the end of our life as we know it.' You hunt around for a little while. The garden, the house. Under his bed and in the wardrobe where he liked to sit and play sometimes. Then down the street. Sick with dread now. You knock on doors. Then you call the police, but by this time he's been gone half an hour and the trail is already cold.

There's a photograph of him my wife Lily and I have kept—it has been our favourite photograph of him, the one which shows him at the age of nine, the one which seemed to us to prove that he was still alive somewhere.

The eyes are mine, the serious mouth belongs to Lily, the pointed chin to my brother Jack. I don't know how they decided on the hair: curly hair that falls over to the left from a small widow's peak. My father is the only one of us who ever had curly hair. His hair was very curly when he was a little boy.

They did the photo when Bobby had been missing for just over five years. We had, I think, all but given up hope when one day, out of the blue, the police rang us and said there was something new they wanted to try.

We thought they'd forgotten all about us, that they had closed Bobby's case, but the next day they came to the house and took away a shoebox full of photos Lily put together for them —photos of Bobby himself along with photos of me, of her, of our parents, of my brother Jack and her sister Carol. All the photos she could lay her hands on of any of us growing up. They studied all the eyes and all the noses; they looked at the thick eyebrows on Lily's side of the family, at the funny widow's peak on mine. They looked at Bobby's four-year-old hairline, at his small round face and our long bony ones, and picked the things they wanted and scanned them into a computer. Then they put everything on a grid and manipulated all the different pieces and stretched Bobby's face until they came up with how he would look if he was nine years old and still alive.

They made leaflets and posters with the new picture on them and, gradually, a few calls started to come in reporting possible sightings, and they began to follow them up.

They cautioned us, though, not to get our hopes up too much; they admitted they couldn't really hold out a great deal of hope. They'd had some success with the photos, but those were cases where the children had been taken by a parent—a mother or a father in a messy divorce. In those kinds of cases putting the new photos out sometimes got a result.

I knew what they were saying. It was what I knew already. It was what Lily knew. That children abducted by strangers are very rarely found alive.

'But,' they said, gently, trying to be kind, 'in our experience the photos can be a great comfort. They can give people something to hold onto.'

When they showed us Bobby's new picture for the first time, we held the precious image in our trembling hands and whispered to each other, 'This could hold us forever.' I watched as Lily touched his curly fringe, very lightly, with the back of her little finger, as if she thought it might be getting in his eyes and annoying him.

'Hello there my darling,' she said, her face breaking into a wondering smile.

We had two large 10" × 8" copies made and framed, one for our bedroom, one for the dining room, an 8" × 5" for my desk at work, some passport-sized ones for my wallet and Lily's purse, so we could take them out and look at them wherever we were, whenever we felt the need—in restaurants, in the car, walking down the street.

Lily began talking to him quite often, telling him all her news. At first this made me uneasy, but after a while I found myself doing it too. Within a few weeks we had both fallen completely under the spell of the new photograph. On his tenth birthday Lily made him a vanilla cake and in front of his framed picture in the dining room, we blew out his candles and made our wish. We forgot the cautious words of the police: for us, the photograph had fixed Bobby in our minds and in the world and made it impossible for us ever to give up hope; it was like a prophecy, a promise that he would come back to us one day and we clung to it—this amazing thing, this beautiful collage they had conjured for us out of our own history, our own flesh and blood.

It is hard for us, now, to know what to do for the best.

He fought them when they found him and took him away from Terri and Shaun Glaister. He bit them and kicked them and clung sobbing to Terri Glaister, his arms around her neck, his fingers locked together so tightly they had to pry them apart one by one.

They found him just over a year after they did the photo and sometimes I wonder how it is they took so long to locate him, because in my opinion his resemblance to the photograph is really quite good, and although the Glaisters did not send him to school, they seem to have taken him out quite a lot.

The chin is wrong, it's true, and the hair—his hair hasn't turned curly in the end the way my father's did at that age; it has remained as soft and thin as it was the day he vanished. But other than that, I think if you ever saw Bobby, if you ever had the chance to compare him with the photograph, you would agree that it is not a bad likeness.

He remembers his blue metal car.

He remembers his blue metal car but he does not remember us.

It is five months now, since he came home, and he still cries for Terri and Shaun Glaister. We have told him, of course, that he can never go back to them. We have explained everything to him, but he says he doesn't care what we say because he hates us.

He is frightened of us too, you can tell. I think we seem very old to him, being as we are so much older than the Glaister couple.

Yesterday he drew himself a picture of them—of Terri Glaister with her short black hair and her narrow face; Shaun with his big hands and big feet, his short red beard. It is not a good drawing, it doesn't much resemble the young elfin-featured woman we saw in the courtroom, nor the bulky man who stood beside her, but it is all Bobby has and it seems to be a comfort to him.

This evening he came downstairs, the picture trailing from his hand, and asked Lily, could he — please — have a frame?

Rose Red

Once, there had been the fisherman and for a while Harlean had sold her memories of him to the red-haired women of the island.

Harlean claimed to have spotted him in the mud one evening, all loose and dead-looking and jostled by the pink, lacy edge of the in-creeping tide; to have put him on her back like a basket of shrimp and carried him home. Harlean (shrunken, old, ugly as a toad) claimed he'd stayed with her till morning, when his friends came in a flat-bottomed boat with a square sail and took him away. She said his hair had been black, and so had that of his friends. 'Black like night,' she'd told the women as they took their coins from their apron pockets and dropped them into the clay dish next to the door.

But after the initial excitement, the women had grown bored. They were tired now of Harlean's story and wondered if it had really happened or was something she'd made up so she could take their money. Harlean still insisted it was true, and when the red-haired women stopped coming, she sat in her little house and looked out at the huge rose-coloured sea and the coral sky and told herself that if he ever came back she would keep him and not let him go. She would put him in the low room under the eaves, bring soft pillows and a lamp in there, and charge them all a shilling a time.

Only Gerda still came whenever she could, with the occasional halfpenny she managed to smuggle out of the crimson tea-pot where Lorm kept the money.

'Tell me again, Harlean,' said Gerda in a whisper, as if she thought Lorm might have followed her along the beach and be listening outside, his thick, rufous beard pressed close against the rough planking of the old woman's little door.

'Go on, Harlean,' she said. 'Tell.' And when Harlean heard the clink of the coin in the dish, she told. The thing about Harlean—greedy, old, ugly Harlean Gill—was that she had a poet's tongue in her frizzled auburn head. To hear Harlean recall the day she found the fisherman was to see him lying across the filthy vermilion quilt of her wooden bed, breathing softly in his sleep and muttering words from his strange language like the lines of a jumbled song. To hear Harlean describe his black hair was to feel it fall across your rust-freckled shoulders; it was to forget, in the cool inky glitter of its touch, the dreary russet monotony of your own people, the red-kissed dot in the ocean where you lived and died.

To Gerda, Harlean's fisherman was a wonder, a cup of water in the desert, as much a miracle as the rainbow that had appeared once in the coral sky when she was a girl, revealing to them all possibilities they had never dreamed of. She confided to Harlean that at night when Lorm was asleep she searched her skin for the coarse red threads his beard had left behind there; she climbed out of bed and crossed the small dark room and dropped them on the fire; watched them sizzle and turn to a pale-pink ash. Night, she said, was her favourite time, when the dark quenched the island of all its lurid pigment and you could look at the black sky and the pale moon and the blinking stars and feel refreshed.

She said she longed for some kind of change, some interruption in the eternal sameness of the island and its inhabitants. She told Harlean how the red dust from the streets coated the inside of her mouth like fur, that she felt thirsty all the time, that she gagged on the shrimp and the ruby-fleshed fish Lorm brought home every night for supper. That she spent hours in the woods hunting for undiscovered leaves and flowers to make new dyes for their clothes, as if by some miracle she might manage to produce a new colour. She cried with fury when everything came out the way it always had, everything the same ancient, familiar shades of raspberry and rust; salmon, carrot, madder, rose. Scarlet shawls and crimson skirts till you were sick of the sight of them. Every object looking back at you out of your own four walls: the quilt on the bed, the teapot, the floor's woven rug, Lorm's clay pipe, his soft work cap, everything washed with the same dull repeated palette.

What she dreaded most was the thought of the children she would one day bear Lorm. She watched the other women kissing and cuddling theirs: all of them, as far as she could see, exactly alike, with the same tedious shock of thick, glowing curls, each one like something grown in the island's glutinous gingery clay and pulled from it. Sometimes she went across to her neighbours' houses to mind the children while their mothers went out on some errand. She could hardly tell one child from the next; the sight of them filled her with an indescribable boredom.

Harlean listened silently, and thought of the income to be had, should the fisherman and his friends or some other freak of nature ever set foot on their shores again.

Lorm knew all about the stolen halfpennies. He'd watched Gerda hurrying past their neighbours' low houses strung along the beach road until she reached the old woman's hovel right at the end. He'd heard the hiss of his own hair in the fire at night and asked himself how he could change to make his wife happy. He knew that his contentment with what they had, with the way things were, was a thorn to her. She couldn't bear him to tell her he had everything he wanted here in the island's pink, pleated cliffs, their russet pigs.

My beloved flame-haired wife.

She ended up storming off to the beach in a fury and he'd watch her from the house, a small strawberry smudge in the distance looking out to sea. He pictured the grim determined set of her square, heavy jaw. It was as if she believed that by the sheer force of her longing, she could change things.

One day, brought to furious tears by a batch of new dye—a deep, nauseating shade of copper that merged with everything around her and made her chest heave—Gerda screamed at Lorm like she never had before. Screamed at the back of his bowed red head bent over the logs as he arranged them carefully into a neat pyramid for their evening fire.

'Aren't you ever curious, Lorm? Aren't you ever thirsty for something new that might be out there?' and she thrust a freckled finger towards the window in the direction of the sea.

Lorm felt her scorn in his back. He was conscious of his own head bobbing in and out of the fireplace as he worked, and thought how he must look like a fat red bird. He turned to look at his wife. Her flushed face was almost the same florid shade as her hair. He thought she looked lovely. He wished he could invent something to long for, but however hard he tried, nothing came into his mind. A hopeless, lop-sided smile slid across his face. He shrugged, extended his empty, spade-shaped hands towards her and she ran out of the house, across the field behind and vanished into the trees.

On the other side of the wood, she stopped running, burning hot and choking. Her hair hung thickly over her arms; she picked up a hank of it, held it up to the light and groaned. The red trees blazed around her, in the water below the pink cliffs she could see shoals of coral fish moving, kicking up the sand beneath them and making it rise through the rosy water in scarlet clouds. A wave of nausea ploughed through her body, she shivered, her limbs shook, her teeth chattered and she sank to her knees. 'God help me,' she whispered and vomited on the ground.

Harlean Gill was sure she'd glimpsed a sail out on the horizon. She was certain she could smell something new and foreign on the breeze.

If she closed her eyes she could picture his cabin, a map spread out on the table, showing a tiny dot in the middle of a great expanse of nothing. She could hear it crackle beneath his exploring fingers. In her mind's eye, she saw his notebooks, his specimen jars, his butterfly nets; she pictured his black hair arranged in a long pigtail, tied with a ribbon half-way down his back. She could see him opening the door of a narrow cupboard where his clothes hung like a rainbow.

She swept out the cramped, windowless room beneath the eaves, put two pillows on the floor in one corner and plumped them up till they looked like a pair of rosy cheeks. Crimson feathers flew out of the seams, turned slow somersaults in the air. She filled a lamp with oil. She was sweating when she'd finished, her dry hair stuck out like a wild auburn hedge, ruby dust rimed her fingernails. Finally, she checked the fit of the key in the roughly gouged lock, wiped the clay dish by the door with a fresh rag and sat down on the doorstep to wait.

Gerda lay in bed with the curtains drawn. She had been almost constantly unwell since the afternoon she'd run off into the woods. She was very quiet, too ill to go to Harlean's. She still tried to picture the fisherman but as the months went by she found it harder and harder without the help of the old woman's poetry. She began to wonder if the other women weren't right after all to say that Harlean had made him up, that such a being could not exist, and they should all forget about the whole thing. What did they want with such a man anyway? they said. They had everything they could ever need right here on the island. Slow tears crept down over Gerda's face, across the broad bridge of her nose and onto her cheeks and down behind her neck into the collar of her nightgown.

'I am so sorry, Lorm', she said sometimes, touching the side of his face with sad affection.

She tried to shut out all thoughts of the future.

'Don't,' she said, when Lorm tried to talk to her about the baby that was coming.

Occasionally she asked him to bring her something to pass the time: the darning egg and a needle and a handful of his worn-out socks. A pot of vegetables to peel. But one afternoon Lorm came home to find her crying again. She had cut her hand with the paring knife and it had bled onto the potatoes.

'See, Lorm,' she said, holding up a potato so he could look. 'There is no difference at all between the colour of my blood and the skin of this potato.'

The blank despair in his wife's eyes made Lorm's heart shrink.

Anxious and wary, he watched her. He emptied the crimson teapot onto the table, letting the coins trickle through his fingers. He picked up a halfpenny, turned it between his thumb and his forefinger, felt its uneven, frilly edge and wondered exactly how many like it his wife had given away already to the greedy, lying Gill woman with her mad stories and her false promises. He counted up all the money they had, arranging it into small piles according to its value. He told himself he would do anything if it would make his wife happy.

As the expected birth approached, he wandered restlessly in the woods and up and down the vacant beach below the single line of low houses where he and Gerda and all the other inhabitants of the island lived, all of them facing the ocean, a row of spectators looking out across an empty stage.

Harlean was nothing if not patient.

While Gerda pined in her bed and Lorm roamed about trying to distract himself from his worries, the old woman waited. She'd come to acknowledge that she'd been mistaken about the explorer being so close, about the sail of his ship already showing itself above the thin red line of the horizon. But she was as sure as she'd ever been that he was out there somewhere. The picture she had of him was as sharp and clear as it had been when it first bloomed in her mind; indeed it had become much clearer over the last few months; it had gathered depth and detail during the long evenings she'd spent sitting waiting in the dark, or moving slowly about in the little room that was prepared under the eaves for his imprisonment. A young man, he would be, well-made and tall—taller than Lorm. Married, no doubt, with a child of his own left behind when he boarded his ship. She saw a picture in a wooden frame of the wife and child—moon-pale and dark-haired just like him—on the small fold-out table he had bolted to the wall of his cabin. He would be a reluctant guest, almost certainly, however great Gerda's charms might be—and Harlean did not consider the young woman's charms to be very great. Lorm's wife, with her firm, slightly jutting jaw, the flatness over the bridge of the nose, was no beauty. Harlean worried the locked door would not be enough. Remembering the thick old chain she had used to hobble her old horse before it died, she scurried down the short open staircase, past her low bed with its ancient vermilion quilt, past the stone-cold hearth, and out by the door to fetch it.

If anyone could have got hold of him, if anyone could ever have conjured him up out of the sea, it would have been Harlean.

Lorm was out when the baby came.

A girl, born quickly and without trouble onto the stone floor early one morning. Still lying on her back, Gerda grasped it beneath its slippery armpits. It coughed and cried and its bandy legs pedaled the air as if it were trying to escape.

Gerda saw Lorm appear in the doorway, saw him stop and drop his soft crimson cap onto the ground and stare, openmouthed.

Gerda stared too at the creature in her hands. She could never have imagined such a thing.

'Look, Lorm,' she said.

Its hair was thick and dense and very red, like her own, like Lorm's beard; its skin freckled like hers with tawny spots, its jaw square and firm like hers too. It had Lorm's shovel-shaped hands. Her flat, broad nose. Gerda's stomach lurched and seemed to empty.

She held their daughter up to the light, showing Lorm the squashed tomato face, the lantern jaw, the shovel hands, the copper thatch of tough, clumpy hair.

Neither of them said a word. Lorm squatted on the floor next to his wife and in the silence they continued to look.

They loved her at once with a fiery passion that lasted all their lives.

The Captain's Daughter

He began, as you might expect, with quite small things. Coming downstairs with half his face unshaved, leaving the gas on when he'd finished cooking, gardening in his bare feet. Within a couple of months, he had adopted a clumsy, shuffling gait; sudden expressions of panic and confusion.

These days he seems worse. He appears frightened now, when I leave the room, a look of startled alarm freezes his features. There are times when we are out in the street when he truly does not seem to know where he is, and if I let go of his arm for two seconds to go and post a letter, or to go and get the Pay & Display sticker for the car, I come back to find him standing next to it, apparently bewildered and afraid, anxiously toeing the gravel with the point of his shoe. One day in the kitchen a while ago he was making one of his Bakewell tarts and he couldn't remember what an egg was.

Then last Thursday morning, he came downstairs without his hand.

He stood in the kitchen doorway, smiling at me. He was fully dressed—socks, slippers, grey wool-mix trousers, clean shirt, cardigan—but he was missing his hand. The shock made me drop my tea cup. It smashed on the kitchen floor, spattering my bare leg with scalding liquid and tiny sharp chips of porcelain.

'Oh for goodness sake, Daddy,' I said, appalled.

I led him back upstairs and he appeared to be genuinely confused and quite distressed to see his hand lying there on the bedside table. He put it on and took my arm and we came back down and had our poached eggs together before Frannie arrived to keep an eye on him and I left for the shop.

On Saturday he wandered off into town by himself to buy potatoes for a shepherd's pie and couldn't find his way home. By chance Dr. Ray saw him standing at the top of the high street and drove him back to our front door.

The hand incident really bothered me.

I have always thought of my father's hand as an integral part of who he is and now it seemed possible that he was quite literally falling apart.

In the old days, before his retirement, it defined him absolutely. You could see it in the eyes of the people who worked for him, that they thought of him as ruthless and hard, a little cruel perhaps, and certainly quite frightening. You could see that none of them liked the feel of his hand—its sudden heaviness, the gloved weight of the softly curled fingers, the unexpected seams in its stitched skin. My father is a big, burly man and although his hand was not necessarily the first thing people noticed about him, it was always what they remembered afterwards. It has always been his trademark—his banner, if you like, his public sign. In those days, it marked him out as the boss, the chief, and I loved that. *A Captain of Industry* my Aunt Wyn used to call him. I loved that he was in charge, that he was powerful and important.

And despite the horrible circumstances in which he lost his real hand, I have never, if I'm completely honest, regretted its loss in the long run. I have always liked its leather-clad replacement. I like its heaviness, its solidity. When I was a little girl I used to love the way it closed like a lid onto the thin ball of my shoulder. Its weight then was the most comforting thing in the world. I loved the sight of my own small fist cupped in his smooth black palm, like a white bud. At school when people asked me about it I used to enjoy telling them it had been bitten off by a crocodile, which shut them up pretty quickly and made them regard me with a kind of shocked envy.

Even in the final years before his retirement, when his power was waning and others—younger men—were jostling to get in there and take his place, it always seemed to me to be the thing that stopped him looking beaten. Even when he came home one day with a slim little box in a plastic carrier bag and said he had decided to do something about his hair which by then had grown sparse and silvery. Even when he stepped out of the bathroom onto the landing wearing an uncertain smile and ludicrously dark, solidly black hair, and some of the dye began to trickle tragically from his left temple into one of the crooked paths in the skin of his face and he looked like poor old Dirk Bogart in *Death in Venice*, sitting in his deckchair beside the lagoon, dying of love and Asian cholera, and I had to say, 'Oh, Daddy, come here, let me clean this off.' Even early the next morning, when he left the house to go to work—when he raised the curved shape of his leather hand against the dusty purple sky to wave to me, I felt sure he would triumph because of it. Tears sprang into my eyes.

'Give 'em hell!' I shouted.

These days Daddy's hand is a rather shabby thing but I still like it—the knuckles are faded and worn like the bald patches on a much-cuddled teddy bear, or an old leather sofa. It has grown old like he has, softer and more comfortable as he has settled into the gentler rhythms of his retirement. His reading, his gardening, his cooking. Our life here in this house.

I found it profoundly upsetting that he could appear in front of anyone, even me, without this part of himself; that he could emerge so incomplete one morning from his bedroom.

Unless he's faking it.

Is that possible?

Peter thinks so.

He thinks Daddy is pretending. He thinks Daddy is a naughty, scheming, selfish, mischievous old bastard who is having us on.

Is that really possible?

Dr. Ray says no, absolutely not. He says there is no way on earth Daddy could be pretending. He says gravely that the prognosis is very poor, that there are rough times ahead and we must be prepared for that.

Peter and I met last summer, a year ago now, and the bizarre thing is that it was Daddy's hand, in a way, which brought us together.

Peter had been walking past the shop and seen the set of Finch, Pruyn Shakespeares I had in the window. He came in and said he wanted to buy them; he said he'd never seen anything like them, he loved all the different colours. I said I liked them too. I would have said anything, really, to get him talking, to keep him in the shop—this tall, thin man with short, thick, toffee-brown hair, untidy in a checked cotton shirt and jeans. Younger than me, I guessed—late twenties, maybe thirty. (In fact Peter is exactly my age, thirty-two).

It was true though, the colours of the plays were pretty—they all looked very handsome in their various linen boxes: *Othello* in purple, *Twelfth Night* in bright lime green, *Hamlet* in black, *Titus Andronicus* ominous in red. I straightened the books into a neat tower, *Titus* on top.

'Ooh,' I said. 'Gory.'

Peter looked blank and that made my heart leap—the thought that his buying the books had been an excuse, a pretext, to come into the shop and meet me, that he'd seen me through the window, sitting in the low armchair behind the little round table in the corner, and decided he had to come in.

'Titus,' I said, tapping the red linen box with the tips of my fingers. 'He chops off his own hand. His enemies tell him that if he sacrifices it he will save the lives of his sons.'

Peter raised his eyebrows.

'And?'

'It's a trick. The old man loses his hand and his sons die any-way. A messenger brings him the boys' severed heads.'

Peter sucked in his breath. 'Ooh,' he said, smiling. 'Gory.'

I laughed stupidly, too loudly. And because I wanted to keep him there, I blurted out the next thing that came into my head.

'My father only has one hand.'

Peter's charming, open smile faded. He tipped his head to one side in a gesture of polite surprise. 'Really?'

I thought he'd go then. After this intimate and unasked-for detail. Unsavoury, possibly even a little grotesque. I cursed myself and waited for him to scoop up his books and make a quick exit, but he stayed and I told him about the night my mother left home and Daddy slammed his fist through a thick pane of glass in the French windows at home. I told him how from my bedroom I heard the tinkle of the glass and went down in my pyjamas to find him crouched in a lake of blood on the lit-tle patio at the back of the house, his hand with its upturned fingers sitting some distance away, like some large pale flower growing up out of the dry soil between the flags; next to it, a huge slab of plate glass, like the blade of a guillotine.

'Jesus Christ,' said Peter.

He stayed. I made us coffee and he sat in the low chair in the corner and watched while I sold six books to four people.

After that everything happened with what I suppose you might call indecent haste. At two-thirty in the afternoon I closed up the shop, threw the tarp over the table of books out on the pavement, and reached for Peter's arm as we ran across the road in front of the traffic, onto the promenade and down the steps to the beach, where I sat behind him, my arms under his cotton shirt against the tight warm skin of his belly.

He asked where I lived. I held his wrist, separated the index finger from the others, moved it along the horizon and down to the coast road.

'There. The little pink house.'

'Just you?'

'Just me and my father.'

Peter has been to the house hundreds and hundreds of times since then. For seven months he has been living with us, and now it seems Daddy can't remember who he is.

We've talked it over several times with Dr. Ray, Peter doing most of the talking. Peter's tack is always the same: aren't all these things my father is doing—the shuffling walk, the fear, the confusion, the memory loss, the egg, his hand for God's sake— aren't they all things he could have read up about, aren't they all the sort of things he knows he's *supposed* to be doing?

Dr. Ray is tired of this line of questioning. Last week in his surgery he leaned back in his chair and folded his arms. He looked weary and irritated. He has known Daddy for years and he seems upset by what's happening.

'And why would he want to do that, Peter?'

'Because he hates me.'

Peter said it with one of his simple, charming smiles. A man stating a self-evident truth that only a fool would not accept. 'He wants to get me away from Lucy. He wants Lucy to stay and me to go. He's trying to scare me away.'

Dr. Ray began collecting his things together—various pens and a half-eaten sandwich, the loose papers scattered across his desk. He in turn had the look of a person speaking to someone who is not quite with it, not quite the full shilling, themselves.

'I don't think so, Peter.'

It's true though, what Peter says about my father hating him.

At thirty-two years old I am still his *darling girl*, his *Lou-Lou*. For twenty-six years it has just been the two of us and that, I suppose, is how he wants things to be.

He has been difficult about Peter from the start. From the very first day I brought Peter home to meet him he has been difficult. I think he sensed immediately that this was it, that Peter was The One. In the months before his behaviour began to change there were already signs—very clear signs—that he would prefer it if Peter were not around. Petty, childish things—

never passing on Peter's phone messages; repeatedly booking only two tickets when I mentioned there was something I wanted to see at the Plaza; cooking only two mackerel when Peter came for supper and making a great drama about dividing them into three portions.

It does seem almost possible now, when Daddy greets Peter with the thin bewildered smile he has acquired lately, that he is only pretending not to know him—that this is part of a plan, a strategy. A kind of mad theory, if you like, that if he behaves as if Peter is a total stranger, as if he has no recollection of ever having met him, then Peter will eventually go away, he will vanish and it will be just the two of us again, together like before.

That, or the belief that if he makes himself troublesome enough, enough of a burden, he will simply frighten Peter away.

Peter and I talk about little else these days.

I have taken to waking him up in the middle of the night to go over some incident that has occurred during the day—the smallest things: a brief moment, for example, when Daddy's drifting stare has seemed to harden, when there is a weird clarity in his eyes and they appear to be fixed malevolently on Peter, and then he blinks and the impression is gone, lost. We talk until the early hours about how curious it is that his symptoms only began around the time that Peter moved in, and how much worse they have become since we started talking about looking for our own place. Again and again we analyse what has become known as 'the tongue incident'—when I caught him in the mirror, sticking his tongue out at Peter, all the way out, like a gargoyle. What sort of action is that? Is that a sign that he has lost all notion of what is appropriate and acceptable behaviour? If so, why was he doing it behind my back? We argue about the £90 a week I'm paying Frannie to come in for a few hours a day to keep an eye on him while Peter's at work and I'm at the shop. Peter says I might as well be flushing the money down the toilet. I say, yes, I know, but I can't bring myself to *not* do it, I can't let go of the possibility that all of this might somehow turn out to be real.

We discuss his cooking.

The chaotic, unkempt, inedible dishes he insists on producing several times a week.

Daddy took up cooking when he retired. He enrolled in a class at the Adult College and found he enjoyed it. He was quite good; he picked up the rudiments easily—a basic white sauce, short-crust pastry, a good chicken stock—and he soon acquired a repertoire of simple dishes: lasagna, shepherd's pie, moussaka, toad-in-the-hole. Shortbread, Bakewell tart, apple crumble. Before long he was cooking for the two of us and in the evening when I came home from the shop there was always some interesting smell coming from the kitchen when I turned in at the gate.

These days his moussaka arrives on the table with the aubergine slices sticking out at odd angles through a stiff floury sauce, all black and crispy and burned. His shepherd's pie comes drowning under a tide of watery gravy spilling up across crazily zig-zagging furrows of mashed potato.

Peter thinks this is the crassest, most ridiculous part of his pantomime. Every horrible misshapen offering—each one of them is deliberate, staged, part of the act. A charade. He says he has known people with this illness and he's sure this isn't what it's like, he doesn't care what Dr. Ray says.

We talk about the times when Daddy is strangely lucid. What are they all about? Why would he suddenly decide to seem okay?

If he were really losing his mind, would he suddenly start talking to me fluently as he sometimes does about the distant and recent past, about his old career, about my schooldays, about how much he still misses my mother? About the rain that hasn't let up since Monday, and how he hates the soft squeaky sound of Frannie's crêpe-soled shoes on the kitchen floor when she's here during the week?

Would he go out into the garden like he did last week and divide the astilbes and replant half of them quite sensibly in the shade beneath the flowering cherry in the front? Would he engage me in a thoroughly normal discussion about what I thought he should try in the area of dry shadow under the bay window by the front door—some Lilyturf maybe?

Would he carry on with his reading? Wouldn't that be something he'd have lost his grip on by now? And yet his appetite is undiminished, voracious and eclectic as it has been all through his retirement. He is always asking Frannie to take him to the library so he can exchange his books for new ones. In the course of the last week he has read *The Warden* and *Framley Parsonage. Get Shorty and Maximum Bob.* Margaret Thatcher's memoirs. *Great Expectations, Catch 22*, and John Keegan's *The Face of Battle.*

Maybe he's heard somewhere that sufferers sometimes experience a kind of reprieve, says Peter. Or maybe he simply can't keep it up all the time, maybe he just decides he wants a break sometimes. Maybe there are some things he just can't bring himself to give up, maybe he's just not a very good actor.

I've spoken to Dr. Ray about these things on the phone. 'Is this unusual?' I've asked him. 'Is it strange that he should have these islands of clarity and competence?'

I can sense the doctor's irritation on the other end of the line. His answer is always the same: that we know very little, really, about exactly how the brain dies.

There are times when I wonder if Dr. Ray isn't in on the whole thing.

This past week, ever since the morning he came down without his hand, my father has been very much worse; he seems to have gone into a very steep decline, a sort of free-fall where he appears to be in a state of almost perpetual bewilderment and anxiety. He clutches my arms when I get up to leave the room for the briefest time, and when I come in he is sitting there on the sofa, very still and upright on the cushions, like a frightened bird.

Today Daddy has been behaving very badly. He refused to get dressed this morning and when I went in to help him he pushed me away quite roughly. He struggled when I attempted to get his vest on over his head. It was very upsetting.

I could feel Peter looking at me.

'Leave him alone for a bit,' he said, taking my hand. 'He'll be down.'

Sure enough, my father appeared about half and hour later. He had dressed himself, after a fashion—shoes but no socks, shirt not properly tucked in—and once again he had neglected to put on his hand.

Peter rolled his eyes.

'Here, Daddy,' I said, pulling out a chair, 'Come and eat some breakfast.'

Later, it being Sunday, we went for a short walk on the promenade, the three of us together, my father in the middle, shuffling along, gripping my arm tightly all the way as if he thought he would fall down and die if he didn't hold on to it.

Back home I put the joint in the oven and laid the table. Dr. Ray had brought over some plums from his garden during the week and Daddy said now that he wanted to make one of his tarts for pudding. Behind his back Peter pulled a face and put a hand to his throat as if he were gagging on something vile.

'You do that, Daddy,' I said. I was exhausted after another night without sleep, picking over with Peter the details of my father's behaviour, looking for all the things that could be deemed suspicious, inauthentic, trying to figure out what's going on, if he's up to something. I said I was going up for a short rest before lunch and left the two of them in the kitchen, Daddy already busy sifting flour into the big brown mixing bowl, Peter putting away the last of the breakfast things. He winked at me, a bright, encouraging keep-your-pecker-up-girl wink, and said he'd bring me up some coffee in a little while.

For a long time I lay on our bed staring at the ridges in the ceiling where one piece of wallpaper overlapped the next. I tried to remember the name of the decorator my father had used for the work and couldn't. All I could remember was how he'd yelled at the poor man afterwards for doing such a terrible job. He shouted so loudly and so furiously that the little decorator had cowered behind his ladder while Daddy told him how useless he was and he wasn't going to pay him a penny. I can see that some people would think my father was quite an unpleasant man.

I couldn't sleep.

I got up and crossed the landing into my father's bedroom at the front of the house. I went to the window and looked out at the clump of astilbes now flourishing in their new position under the cherry tree. After a while I turned to look back at his room.

There was the usual chaos. The bedcovers askew. Mismatched shoes lined up next to his wardrobe. A jumble of assorted items next to the lamp on his bed-side table—a comb and a few biscuits, a sock, his hand. Roy Jenkins' biography of Churchill. *Lieutenant Hornblower*. Peter's copy of *Titus Andronicus* in its red linen box.

I picked up the *Titus*.

It made me sad, holding it, thinking of the afternoon Peter stepped into the shop for the first time, before any of this business with my father began. I slipped the book out of its red box and took it back with me to my room. I lay down on our bed and began to read. It struck me now as rather a bad play, absurdly violent and full of moments of unintended comedy. I wondered, as others have, if Shakespeare could really have written it; if there was any way you could ever play it other than for the laughs.

I'd forgotten quite how gruesome the ending is, what a grisly, over-the-top finale Act Five serves up: the old man slaughtering his daughter's seducers and baking them in a pie.

Oh honestly.

For goodness sake.

From out in the hall I could hear the radio on the other side of the kitchen door. I could hear the pulsing hum of the Vent-Axia, the spitting of the joint in the oven. There was a rich, meaty smell. I went in.

Daddy was crimping the pastry edge of his tart with a fork, very slowly and carefully, like some one learning to do it for the first time. The pie itself looked like a sort of strange hat with a raised brim, collapsed and squashy in the middle and made of a kind of thick wet lace, decorated with glossy, purplish fruit.

There was no sign anywhere of Peter. I stared at the pie. At my father. A long elastic thread of pendulous drool hung over the pie from his open mouth, rising and falling slowly with his breathing.

'Daddy?' I said, but he did not look up.

'Lucy?'

I turned round. It was Peter. Just stepping out from inside the pantry, a bag of potatoes in his hand. He gave me a cheery smile, went over to the counter and began pouring the coffee.

'There you go,' he said, passing me a cup.

My father didn't seem to be aware that I had come into the room.

I touched his arm and he looked at me and he didn't appear to know who on earth I was.

'Daddy,' I said. 'It's me. Lou-Lou.'

He mouthed the word several times. He seemed distressed and muttered it aloud, over and over again, this name that no one but him has ever called me in my entire life.

Then at last he seemed to drift off into a sort of empty day-dream and after another minute or so, he went back to his pie.

All through lunch I could feel Peter watching me. Daddy ate like a baby, dribbling bits of food on his shirt and on his chin.

He's faking it. I know he's faking it.

I look at Peter now, and for a long time we hold each other's gaze. I look from Peter to my father and I don't know what to say. I don't know what to do; his mean, miserly love breaks my heart.

Pied Piper

Mary Owen found the baby in the sand on the afternoon of her
forty-sixth birthday, a Tuesday. She stepped off the bus in the
usual place and walked slowly towards the dunes—very slowly,
Mary Owen being by this time a vast and sluggish woman. She
left her shoes where she always left them, in the shadow of the
wooden turnstile, and continued down towards the beach
beyond, the blue plastic bucket for the cockles swinging off
the crook of her elbow.

She always came on Tuesdays to look for cockles. She'd devel-
oped a yen for them, dressed in vinegar and eaten with a spoon.
(We used to say she was gobbling up her own bitterness with
each sour bowl.) Sometimes, the local boys came up from
Ogmore to watch the fat lady with her blue bucket, her cotton
dress tucked up around her great thighs, bent over the wet sand
in search of the little creatures. But today no one had come to
watch. Even by Ogmore standards, the grey sea was uninviting.
The occupants of a green car were already too far away to
observe Mary, and in another moment, their car had disappeared altogether along the curving road to the east, in the
direction of Southerndown. Which only left the gulls, and the
sheep, nibbling the tarmac in the car park up above the big flat
rocks. Mary walked unseen between the clumps of bloomless

thistles, crunching the coarse grass under her soft, fat feet, until she came to the edge of the dunes and the beginning of the hard strand where the cockles would be. She was, in spite of the cool of the day, red-faced and perspiring. She stopped to fan herself with the lip of the blue plastic bucket, and there, almost at her feet, where the wind had blown a hollow in the sand, was the baby, waiting for her.

Waiting for her—that's how she thought of it. She'd always believed (in spite of everything her mother had told her) that life should be fair, and it hadn't been fair to her. She was sad and disappointed, and we all said it was disappointment that had made her fat. At twenty, she'd been a slip of a girl, but then she'd married Will, who loved her but couldn't seem to give her a baby, and slowly she began blowing up. Every year, thick new layers of herself settling around her resentful heart like the rings of an ageing tree. Her face hadn't changed so much—it was much the same face Will had fallen in love with twenty-six years before. It was recognisably the face of the girl in the photo on the gate-legged table in the Owens' front room. It was only, now, slightly overwhelmed by its surroundings, and there was a look of shock in the round blue eyes, shock at the way life had turned out. The look Mary had was not unlike the small face you see on a coconut, full of sadness and surprise.

Later, watching the Tuesday sun sink behind the mountain, Will would wonder how his wife could go off on the number 12 bus with only cockles on her mind and come back with a baby. But he was wrong, of course, about his wife's mind. Childlessness had ferried Mary into another world. She was ill, wasn't she? Ill with craving.

The baby, a boy, was still mucky from its birth and daubed all over with sand. His skin darkish under its redness, his hair fair in the places where it had been dried by the wind. He was quiet—only his arms flailed in the salted air, as if he thought he were falling and was trying to hold onto something. He was wrapped in a length of clean, white linen which the breeze from the distant water had blown into loose coils around him. More sand blew in gentle gusts off the sloping dune, and had begun to drift softly against him in the hollow. It occurred to Mary that with a little more wind, he might have been quite buried in the sand if she hadn't come. It occurred to her that she'd been guided to this place.

Even so, crouching uncomfortably over the infant, she hesitated. She caught the sour scent of her own anxiety in the air. Grains of sand clung to her warm cheeks. Smooth and unlined in spite of what she'd had to put up with, they had grown slick in the cool sunshine. It was a long time since she'd taken anything that didn't belong to her and tried to keep it as her own. As a girl, she'd taken things. She had a longing for the nice things other people had in their houses, like Ruth Pritchard's mum's jewelry (a jet necklace and a gold ring set with a huge, milky opal). The Pendelphin rabbits Mrs.Bessant had sitting on doilies in her front window. Daffodils from the Gaynors' garden. But Mary's mother had always discovered her daughter's crimes. She'd reminded Mary of the Commandments. *Thou shalt not covet. Thou shalt not steal.* Even the daffodils had to go back, laid on the flowerbed in the Gaynors' small garden with a note of apology tucked into the wet soil. The only stolen thing Mary had ever managed to keep was the chocolate she took once from the Co-op at the bottom of the hill, and that was because she ate it straightaway, wolfing it down in gulps behind her hand, right outside the shop on the pavement before anyone could come and make her take it back.

It plagued her now, the idea that she'd only be allowed to borrow the baby, that one day she'd have to give him back. While she continued to stoop, and to hesitate, a gust of wind tugged at the length of white linen around the baby and it unfurled like an escaping kite until only a corner remained secured beneath the boy's tiny, flat feet. Mary saw then that the piece of linen resembled a tablecloth, embroidered along one edge. Where it was hoisted high into the air by the wind, she saw there was a half-embroidered flower, one blue petal and the toothed edge of a leaf. A needle, and a length of blue silk thread, fluttering from the spot where a second petal had been begun next to the first. She'd rather this had not been the case. She would rather the linen had been a piece of rag, or an old sheet, because she was no fool. She knew, as she stood there in the cool sunshine, that there's a tendency among babies abandoned at birth—babies tucked into bull rushes, babies cast upon the barren flanks of mountains—to come swaddled in invisible complications. And the cloth, with its piece of interrupted sewing, struck her then as a possible complication.

But there was nothing in the whole world she'd ever wanted as much as she wanted this half-buried boy. In the chilly, rising wind, he pursed his blue-brown lips against the dry whipping of the sand. His wrinkled face, not much bigger than an orange, puckered and prepared to cry. He repeated the frantic flailing with his arms in the air. She couldn't help herself. Her hot, swollen heart was pushing up into her throat, telling her that this baby was a thing she was meant to find and to keep. Quickly, she gathered him into her large hands, and carried him, bound warmly now in the tablecloth, back up over the dunes. At the turnstile she slipped her shoes back on and walked carefully up the road to the bus stop.

It takes about an hour on the bus from the beach at Ogmore to our town in the valleys—one bus to Bridgend, then another to bring you the rest of the way. The bus still carries you in the same way it brought Mary that day—past the Co-op at the bottom of the hill, then up between the two matching rows of terraced houses that face each other along the steep slope of the narrow street. The bus comes slowly, it lolls and staggers between the changing of the gears, and looks as if it might start rolling backwards all the way down to the sea. The children said it went extra slowly on a Tuesday with Mary Owen inside it. God, they were noisy weren't they, our children? We had to clamp our hands over their mouths in case she heard.

Half way up, through a gap in the terrace, Mary could see over to the coal mine and, off to the side, the slag heap. The slag—the dark mound of coal waste spat out by the pit—rose up against the green and purple mountain behind our town. All her life, Mary had watched it get bigger every year, up there on the hillside above the school. By the summer of her forty-sixth birthday the slag had grown to be practically a mountain by itself, which some people said they could hear groaning and shifting in the night, as if it were trying to get comfortable.

Our town hasn't changed much to look at since that day. There is the Co-op, and the mine, and the bus stop still in the same place between the Blue Lady and Jerusalem chapel. Only the slag is gone, and the school is in a different place. There is a quiet too, which is new. It is quiet as Hamelin in our little town.

At the stop, between the pub and the chapel, Mary climbed slowly down onto the pavement. Her big hands shook as she walked, she hardly trusted herself to keep the baby safe now she'd got him almost to the maroon door of her own house. She'd been considering, on the bus, how one day she would tell her little boy the secret of his birth. Present him with the mysterious cloth, like a birth certificate. The thought was still there as she stood by the fire in the front room (they always had a fire, even in summer), the piece of linen with its half-done pattern of leaves and flowers lying across her open hands. It was still there when she mounted the narrow stairs to her bedroom, and when she lifted the big, bowing mattress of the old bed, and placed the folded cloth underneath. But by the time she'd gone back into the kitchen, the thought had slipped quietly away. He was hers now.

She stood for a while, looking at the boy where he lay in her own front room, warm and clean and wrapped in a fresh pillowcase and sleeping in the lap of Will's chair. His hair was very fair now she had washed him in the green Fairy soap. She walked back over to the sink where she'd bathed him, and pushed the sandy water down into the plug-hole with the palms of her hands. She wiped the deep sink all round with a dishcloth until there was no trace of the beach left. From the folds of her wrists and her elbows, and the moist spaces between her fingers, she picked away the last grains of sand. When it was all done, she took up the baby again in her arms and sat down in Will's chair by the fire, exhausted from her labours.

There were parties, that evening, when we were told that Mary Owen had given birth to a baby boy on the beach at Ogmore-by-Sea. In the lounge bar of the Blue Lady, the men began toasting the sudden baby before they even noticed Will was there, sitting quietly in the corner, sipping his pint. Talk of a new baby had drifted towards him from the bar, and he'd wondered whose it might be, and then they were dragging him up to the bar, ribbing him about the lead in his little pencil and calling him an old bugger. 'You dark horse. You old dog,' growled Frank Gaynor, the colliery manager, thumping Will's thin back inside its soft brown jacket. His eyes watered and the air seemed to catch inside his narrow throat so that he couldn't speak. When the others were too drunk to notice, he slipped back into his corner and sat there, pressed hard against the bench seat, like a folded shadow. He stared into his pint. He took small, ferrety sips of it, and blushed like a bridegroom. He knew his wife was lying.

Poor Will, he thought he was the only one who knew, but the truth was, we all knew. Everyone knew all along that she must have made the story up but nobody said so. The men knew it when they wet the baby's head that night with seven hundred pints of Brains bitter. And the women—we knew when we went piling into Mary's front room with all our make-shift presents. Talcum powder and cotton sunhats, booties and blankets, all the stuff we had lying around at home. I gave her Huw's Christening frock and she gave me a kiss for it, sweetly scented with the sherry we were drinking out of tea cups, marzipan crumbs on her lips from the Battenberg some one had brought along for the celebration.

You could say there was a conspiracy from the very beginning. Nobody laid their hand on Mary's thick arm and said gently, 'Now, Mary . . .' We went further, said it was the pregnancy that had given her the yen for the sour cockles. Even young Dr. Clare, who surely should have known better, went along with it, arriving at Mary's house without his black bag, as if he'd already made up his mind not to look into things too closely. We all wanted her to be happy, you see, to have what she wanted, to have what the rest of us had. It was only fair. I remember leaving her house that night, looking back into the room, and seeing Mary by the fire, the baby looking so warm and peaceful on her huge pillowed chest you almost wanted to climb up there yourself and go to sleep.

Would she have tried to pull off such a preposterous lie if she hadn't been so enormous? Probably, yes, I think she would have. She began to forget she'd found a stranger's baby in the sand. She began to believe the story she told, how she'd lain down in the coarse grass and with three long and agonising pangs, pushed out the boy she hadn't even known was inside her.

She called him Thomas. Mr. Davies, our minister, baptised him in the chapel. Mary dressed him in Huw's frock.

Thomas Owen became part of our town. For a year he rode up and down the hill in a navy-blue Silver Cross pram. When he was three, Mary bought him his first pair of Startrite sandals, the red ones with the pattern of holes in the toe, the ones she'd lusted after, the ones she'd seen the other mothers buying, paying the extra because it was worth it, because you got the proper fitting. And there was the picture on the box she liked too, with the two Startrite Children, safe in their good shoes even though to Mary they looked as if they were heading off on their own into a dark wood.

Thomas had flat, narrow feet, like Will. 'Look,' Will said to Mary one evening when the boy was in the bath, 'he has my feet.' It always happened like that to Will—by the time the words in his head got out across his lips, they had knitted themselves into different shapes. He said the things Mary liked to hear and kept his worry to himself.

He pictured a fairground girl, a freckled creature with oily hair falling onto her blouse. A dull patterned skirt like the ones worn by the gypsies who used to camp under the lime trees by the river when his mother was alive. The girl had something of the look of the Blue Lady too, who had gold earrings and swung on the painted sign over the pub door. At night she wormed her way into his sleep, searching frantically through her pockets for the thing she had lost. Sometimes a hank of her hair blew against her mouth, and when Will woke, in the night, he felt the girl's matted hair on his own parched lips, dry and salty, and staggered out of bed to fetch a glass of water, past his sleeping wife and baby. When he climbed back into bed his thin body shifted itself about for hours before he finally fell asleep again. He knew nothing then of the folded length of linen with its half-embroidered flower lying buried beneath the mattress, but in the mornings he woke with all his bones aching, as if something hard had got into his dreams and turned him black and blue. He felt sure he would know her if she ever came looking.

When Thomas was four years old, Mary bought him a leather satchel from Howell's in Cardiff and he went to school with the rest of our children, a hundred and twenty-three of them in the low brick building under the slag. Another year passed, and a second, and Thomas Owen turned six.

It is strange to hear a sound and not know what it is or where it is coming from. It began softly, but seemed from the start to be very close—so close that at first, I looked for it in my kitchen.

In his house next to the chapel, Mr. Davies, the minister, heard it too. He paused in his writing. There it was—a low grumbling, and a gentle shifting, which became a roar. A vast deep moan of protest that seemed to rise up from the bottom of the world and come shuddering through his soul.

Through the bedroom window, Mary saw the slag move. The whole mountain seemed to swell, and then to billow, and to burst open and pour down in a filthy deluge onto the school. She watched as all the men in the town came swarming up over the muck. She watched them digging for the children. She gaped at the women standing about in small groups, very still and quiet, as if they'd had their hearts plucked out.

She shrank from the window, trembling and sick. The water in the glass on the dressing table still quivered. In the narrow bed, less feverish than he'd been in the morning when she'd decided to keep him home from school, Thomas slept on.

Another minister had to come to help us with the funerals because Mr. Davies couldn't do it. On the first Sunday after it happened he stood up in our chapel in front of the whole town and held out his arms to us as if he had something to give us, but then he put them down again without speaking and gathered up his pages of foolscap paper and went out through the big chapel doors, leaving us with nothing but the echo of his polished shoes clicking across the stone floor.

He didn't come back into the chapel after that, and spent his days at home, coming out from time to time to fetch bread and milk from the Co-op.

I began to cook for him. I took him hot soup and a bit of pie a few times a week, though more often than not he wouldn't eat them, and we would just sit by the fire in his quiet front room while he ate his loaf from the bag and drank the cream off the milk when it was still in the bottle. Sometimes he said he was very sorry that he had nothing to say to me, but that when your faith has disappeared into the mountain with a hundred and twenty-two children, it is probably better to shut up and be quiet.

On Sundays in chapel Thomas sat between his parents in a new black suit and you could see, in Mary's little coconut face, that all her peace had gone, and that she remembered now what she'd done. People couldn't help looking at Thomas. We all sat with our empty hands folded in our laps, and looked. Everyone seemed to be watching him all the time. It was like a hunger. Mary felt it, and began to hide her golden-haired boy away. One night, she went with Will to see Mr. Davies, and in front of both of them she poured out the details. How she'd found him and wrapped him up like a birthday present to herself and kept him. How in her mind the two things, her theft of the baby and what had happened to our town, had become connected. *Thou shalt not covet. Thou shalt not steal.* What was she after? Forgiveness? Whatever it was, she didn't find it in the minister's house because he had nothing to tell anybody anymore, he was lost for words.

The Owens have left our town. I saw them climb on the bus at the stop between the Blue Lady and the chapel. I could see Thomas's fair head, like a bright coin against the grey stone of the buildings. I watched the bus through the window until it disappeared.

Mr. Davies is gone now, too. I miss cooking for him. To pass the time, I come down to the beach at Ogmore and sit here in the prickly dune grass, looking out across the empty sand, the puckered water. I have been trying, these last few days, to dig a hole, but it's hard work, digging a hole in a sand dune, because the sand keeps running endlessly back through your empty fingers like dry salt. Sometimes, the local boys come up to the beach. When they pass close the dunes, their high voices distract me briefly from my digging. Then they go running off up the beach and leave me to it again, calling to each other, and glancing back over their shoulder at the funny looking woman on the dune—the sad lady from the valleys, digging for babies in the sand.

Boot

I'd misled him, apparently.

I'd confused him.

Everything I'd done, they explained, had combined to encourage him in his delusions.

Apparently I should never have fed him straight from my plate; I should never have given him my bacon rind, my left-over roast potatoes, the fatty ends of my lamb chops. I should never have thrown him peanuts from my handbag as we strolled down the hill to the beach.

Apparently it made him feel important.

Apparently I should never have let him ride in the front seat of the Renault, or on the raincover of the baby's pram and let him poke his big shoe-shaped face inside the dark hood and lick the baby's face with his dry raspy tongue. Apparently it made him think he *owned* us, it made him think we *belonged* to him. I should have stopped him—they explained—when he lunged at the people who came over to say hello, or to admire the baby. I should have grabbed him when he launched himself off the raincover, I should have yanked on his collar when he started racing round my legs and the wheels of the pram in a huge swerving protective parabola of flashing orange fur and yellow teeth. *Heel!* I should have said when he chased cars and bicycles and far-off noises and anything else that seemed to threaten the safety of his little family.

I should have insisted he stay on his blue wool cushion in the corner of the kitchen when he was in the house; I should never have allowed the snare-drum patter of his feet to follow me across the parquet floor of the hall into the sitting room. I should not have permitted him to lie on the sofa, to spend his afternoons lounging among the cushions with me and the baby.

Above all, I should never have allowed him upstairs at night.

I should never have let him spread his long wolfish body across the threshold of our bedroom, I shouldn't have stooped to stroke his sunken flanks on my way to the bathroom while he lay there, snoring softly and blinking his narrow yellow eyes. It only encouraged him. *No*, I should have said, on the nights when Ian's work took him out of town, and he started creeping into our bed, stretching out in the empty hollow on Ian's side. *No*, I should have said, because when Ian's taxi brought him home from the airport very early one morning, and he tried to slip into bed next to me, Boot didn't like it, he didn't like it at all.

We had two options, said Ian, tight-lipped and white with shock.

Either we took Boot in hand—firmly, properly in hand—or we drove him back to the pound that afternoon.

I nodded.

I'd finished washing Ian's wound and it was dressed now in a clean gauze bandage. I looked over at Boot, still sprawled on our bed amid the mangled sheets, smiling and panting a little.

'Maybe we could try taking him in hand,' I said.

Ian said he'd make some phone calls, find out what to do.

Everyone he spoke to said the same thing—that I'd been much too soft with Boot, that I had confused him and misled him into thinking he was important, into thinking he was in charge. As one of them put it, I had misled Boot into thinking he was Ian.

They told us what we needed to do.

We were to give him only dog food—just biscuit and a very little meat—once a day. He was to sleep on his blue cushion in
the corner of the kitchen and he was *never* to be allowed
upstairs. He was banned from the sofa; there were to be no more
pram rides; no more sitting in the front seat of the car; no more
peanuts on our walks down to the beach.

On the advice of an old college friend who was now a vet's
assistant, Ian borrowed his sister's cat, Beulah, and let her eat
from Boot's bowl whenever she felt like it. From the pet shop
next to the bus station he procured a long-haired black and
tan guinea pig which he took out of its cage twice a week in
the evening when he came home from work so it could take a
stroll along Boot's deluded puffed-up spine and remind him
that in the new pecking order, he came last, right at the bottom
of the pile—lower than Ian, lower than me, lower than the baby,
lower than Beulah, lower than the fat piebald guinea pig.

For a while, Boot tried to fight back. There was the odd skir-
mish with the cat; once or twice he swung his head round and
snapped at the strolling guinea pig. Early on, he would sometimes raise his nose from the cold kitchen floor and look up at
me beseechingly with his sad watery eyes as if he thought there
might be a roast potato or the fatty end of a lamb chop still
going, but all he ever got now was a sharp kick from Ian to
remind him of his place in the world.

Boot changed.

By the end of a few weeks he was a different animal. Quiet,
docile, humble. He slept obediently on the kitchen floor. When
I came down in the mornings, he just lifted his shoe-shaped
nose in a sort of muted, gentle greeting. He lost his twitchy, neu-
rotic look when people came up to me and the baby in the
street. He no longer launched himself into a wild, jealous helter-
skelter around the pram whenever there was some unwelcome
distraction—a new face, an approaching car, a strange noise.

He was like an old man.

On Sundays, if the weather was good, we loaded up the Renault
and drove the short distance to the beach—Ian at the wheel,
the baby next to him in her car seat, me in the back with the

towels and the rolled-up windbreak, the deckchairs, the rug, the picnic; Boot on the floor at my feet with the baby's bucket squashed down hard on top of his head.

Usually we set up somewhere not far from the water's edge, and that's what we did on the Sunday I'm remembering now. We set up the deckchairs and the windbreak and laid out the tartan rug. I dressed the baby in her yellow swimsuit, the one with a ruffle like a ballerina's, and I watched her go crawling about after crabs and shells and bits of seaweed to pop. Ian went for a swim and I went to the kiosk for an ice cream and then I settled down in one of the deckchairs to eat it.

A short distance away from me Boot was lying by himself on the sand.

The tartan picnic rug was of course too good for Boot.

I knew that. I'd been told.

'Give Boot an inch,' Ian reminded me nearly every day over breakfast, 'and he'll take a mile.'

I watched him lying there, meek and quiet, scarcely flinching when the baby began sprinkling handfuls of cold pebbles on his back and trying to bury his tail in the wet sand. If he was aware of her, he gave no sign; he just lay on his side like a vegetable, gazing blankly out across the water.

What can I say?

Only that it killed me to see him like that. Only that I knew I liked him better the way he was before, that I preferred things the way they used to be, and that there had always been more than two options.

Ian was a while in the water.

I remember watching him come walking out through the shallow waves, the surf fizzing around his knees, then his ankles. I remember how he started jogging when he reached the dry sand, shouting when he was still quite a long way off.

'What's happening Nicky? What's going on?' he was saying, a little breathlessly because he was running quite fast now, his head tilted to one side, his face scrunched up in an expression of bewildered concern, but by then Boot was already on the rug, half way through his Cornetto and I wasn't really listening.

Scouting for Boys

I'd never liked Needham.

He was small and thin with hollow cheeks and a pointed chin, a mole like a film star near his cramped little mouth. His head was shaved and you could see the bone of his skull where it joined his neck. It made the shape of an *m*, the same shape young children draw to show a bird in the sky. In school I used to stare at it from my seat, directly behind him because my surname followed his, so close I could have reached out and run my finger along that ridge of bone there, along the seam of his head.

His eyes were grey and narrow and inscrutable, like the rest of his pale sharp face. You knew he'd never explain to you why there was just him and his grandmother at home, and a dark-skinned little girl who was supposed to be his sister but looked nothing like him. None of us knew his story, he kept it locked up inside himself, inside his closed-up little heart, inside the small, bony scaffold of his head.

I didn't like him. He had grime under his fingernails and a rude, aggressive manner, and on the one occasion I'd tried to do him a kindness, he'd shown no gratitude whatsoever. I'd found a book of his on the path on my way home one afternoon and, knowing where he lived, I took it to him.

I could see his place, a shabby little flat over somebody else's shop, from my house. I could see it in the distance on the other side of the park, beyond the high creosoted fence and the glittering screen of poplars there.

A short metal staircase led up to a concrete porch and a hollow wooden door with a straight handle. His grandmother answered when I knocked. She was small like Needham and had the same pinched angular features. She was dressed in a droopy flesh-coloured dressing gown with a man's striped tie for a belt. On her head, beneath a see-through lemon scarf, I could see a few wisps of white hair, soft and flyaway like a baby's. She looked me up and down, her eyes travelling slowly over my blue school coat, my brown shoes.

I gave her Needham's book. She took it without looking at it and carried on looking all over me, at my coat, my legs in their grey school trousers, my shoes. She moistened her lips, as if seeing me had made her hungry. She had the same hard look as Needham but her voice when it came was soft and slow and vague.

'Are you going to wait for him?'

I had no intention of waiting, of going inside or staying, but she had already turned to lead me in. As I followed her, I could see through the gauzy scarf on her head and the sparse white fluff of her hair that she had the same ridge of bone at the base of her head as he did. Where it made him look stubborn, it made her look fragile, brittle. It looked like a fault, a fissure, a place you could tap and it would crack open and show you what was in there.

There was no hallway. The door opened immediately into a room which was part kitchen and part bedroom, there were three narrow beds spread with thin nylon sleeping bags against one wall. On the other side of the room stood a gas stove with two burners.

There was no wardrobe and there were no cupboards, the only place where anything could have been stored was in a little red suitcase which stood all by itself in one corner.

One door led off the room. Through it I could see a low yellow bath draped with a balding green hand-towel, a pattern of glue on the wall behind where tiles had once been. There was no sign of Needham's dark-skinned little sister. There was a smell of fishpaste and digestive biscuits.

Without asking if I wanted it, Needham's grandmother made me a horrible cup of powdered coffee with dried milk. I drank it in silence, and then Needham came in through the door.

'This boy brought your book back,' said his grandma in the same sweet dreamy voice as before. I wondered if she drank. She smiled at Needham as if she couldn't see what had happened to his pale face when he saw me in there, hadn't seen it turn even harder and tighter than usual. I'd never seen him look so mean.

Needham ignored her and didn't say a word when I handed him his book. He stood stiffly near the door and watched while I drank the horrible coffee. It tasted of chicory and sand and I wished I hadn't come. I didn't want to be there. I wanted to be away from this strange dirty boy, his odd family, his rude challenging stare. I drank as much of the foul coffee as I could and then I left.

Needham had never come with us to camp before that summer.

It was a shock to see him there that morning, waiting on the pavement in front of the park for the coach. It was a shock to see him coming with us, Needham who lived, not in a house, but in a shabby little flat over some one else's shop, whose sister looked nothing like him. Needham who wore on his feet black elasticated plimsoles instead of shoes. Needham who always wore the same stale pair of washed-out grey shorts, whose green scout's shirt looked like something he'd made himself, whose grandma drank and drifted about in an ancient dressing gown in the middle of the day.

The morning we left for the Lakes he was there before anyone, standing on his own waiting for the coach. He was wearing his usual clothes: the plimsoles, the washed-out shorts, his peculiar home-made scout's shirt. The thin navy mac he sometimes wore to school hung from his hand. The only thing that was different about him was that he looked, in an anxious sort of way, rather happy. He shifted about excitedly on the thin rubber soles of his plimsoles, craning his neck to see if the coach was coming yet.

He was smiling, and he had brought with him the most extraordinary bag.

It was the little red suitcase I had seen in the corner of his grandmother's flat, made out of molded plastic with a metal lock beneath a long handle. It was the most completely unsuitable thing, and drew attention to itself almost monstrously as it sat there upright on the pavement in the place where the rest of us had heaped our drab green and brown rucksacks.

His blue sleeping bag was all right. There was nothing really wrong with that, it was only rather thin and grubby. He'd tied it round with string and it did not really stand out from the others in the pile. I recognised it from my visit to his home.

But the suitcase shocked me. It was like a cheap version of something my mother might use, a coarse copy of the leather week-end case she used for short trips away with my father, the sort of case that had a shiny fabric lining and a ruched pocket for brushes and combs and an oblong mirror set into the lid. I'd watched my mother pack hers on several occasions. I'd watched her take her cosmetics out of the bathroom cabinet— her Helena Rubinstein Washing Grains, her Revlon moisturiser, the round cake of Roger & Gallet soap in its green opaque box. I'd watched her zip them into her sponge bag and put the bag in the suitcase with her nightie, her underwear, her Carmen rollers. I'd seen her turn the small, flat key in the lock beneath the handle, and carry it down to the car.

Some of the boys laughed openly at Needham's red suitcase.

'Nice bag, Needham,' said Qualtrone.

But Needham raised his pointed chin and ignored him, he looked steadily at the approaching coach as if all he was thinking about were mountains and rivers and fires, and all the things we were going to be doing in the Lakes, all the things he'd heard us talk about over the years but had never yet experienced for himself. Mr. Persian arrived then and we loaded everything on, and the others seemed to forget about the little plastic case.

It disturbed me though, this woman's bag of Needham's, with its long handle and its lock, and its suggestion of lace and stockings and perfumed soap.

We all thought of Mr. Persian as an old man, but I see now, when I conjure again his broad open face, that he was young.

He had dark, almost black hair, which he wore smoothed with Brylcreem close to his scalp, and parted in a clean white line on the left side. He was short and powerful, always very smart and neat in his uniform.

A scout is clean.

He reminded us often of this and it had always been a mystery to me how he could tolerate someone as slovenly and ill-kempt as Needham when he was himself so careful about his appearance and ours. Only Mr. Persian's fingernails let him down—he was ashamed of them, I think—they were chewed to the quick and didn't belong to the rest of him. They were the hands of another man and he hid them away whenever he could in the pockets of his shorts.

We all liked him very much. We liked him better than our teachers, who were sarcastic and bored and didn't seem to enjoy being with us. Many of us, I think, liked him better than our fathers, I certainly liked him better than mine. I think I liked Mr. Persian, actually, at that time, more than anyone else in the world. I liked the fact that he seemed to enjoy being with us, that he talked to us. I liked the seriousness with which he went about everything we did together, as if all of it—a good star-shaped fire, the right knot, the difference on a map between a mixed wood and an orchard—were real life, as if it mattered much more than anything else we did in the rest of our lives, as if it were more real than school and the time we spent with our families, more real than whatever it was he did when he was not with us on Thursday evenings in the white hut on the Forest Road, and in our one week away together in the summer.

It was his custom to give us all a copy of the handbook when we joined. I still have mine, the green and red 1967 paper-back edition, and while I can see now that it is, on the whole, a self-important, rather comical little book, both priggish and prurient, at the time I was very proud of it, wrote my name in ink on the flyleaf, and committed great chunks to memory. To this day I can remember that the span of my extended arms is almost equal to my height. I can remember that a line through the belt and head of Orion will give you the Pole Star.

That the best way to harden the feet is to soak them in a solution of water and alum.

That a poisonous snake carries its venom in a bag concealed within its mouth.

Every day that we were away it was warm and sunny except for the last one when we did our big climb and it rained. We did all the usual things during the week that summer, the same as any other: we hiked up to Grisedale Tarn, and took the ferry across Ullswater to Pooley Bridge. We took a bus into Penrith and visited Brougham castle.

Until the end, only one small incident marred everyone's enjoyment of the week—a nasty scuffle quite near the beginning between Qualtrone and Needham when Qualtrone made some remark about Needham's sister which Needham found offensive. The result was a short, scrappy fight during which Qualtrone had his cheeks viciously raked by Needham's fingernails. Mr. Persian broke them apart with his usual brisk composure, he didn't shout at them, he just sent them off in different directions to perform various chores and that was that.

Otherwise Needham looked very happy. I don't think any of it disappointed him. He kept up with Mr. Persian on our walks, half running all the time, like some lean and hairless dog, to keep up with the older man's smart pace. He seemed hungry to hear about everything there was to see. Whenever you looked, Needham was up there at the front of any group when Mr. Persian stopped to point something out. This is how it was all the time on our walks; it seemed to me he was always, always there, right at the front with Mr. Persian, almost beside himself with the pleasure of it all.

All through our walks Mr. Persian kept up a stream of observation as we went along. He prided himself on his sharp eyesight, on his ability to read the landscape spread out before us: *a scout is observant*, he liked to say.

He maintained this constant patter as we walked, holding up his short muscular arms from time to time as a sign for us to stop when he saw something he particularly wanted us to notice, to learn from. I can still picture him, striding out in front, the smooth unspooling of his commentary. *Trig Point. Oxbow Lake. U-shaped Valley. Mica Schist. Victorian Spruce Plantation. Limestone Pavement.*

One day we found rapsberries growing by the path and ate them with our sandwiches. Needham ate his sitting on the ground next to Mr. Persian. I can see them now, Needham is smiling, they both are, sitting there together, with Mr. Persian looking happy too, leaning back with his knees clasped in his hands, relaxing in the rare, new sunshine of Needham's smiles. From time to time Mr. Persian would say something that made Needham laugh and then you saw his pale unwholesome face open like a flower.

On another occasion—a hot afternoon later in the week—we went swimming in a deep hole at the foot of the mountain where we had set up our camp. The water was icy and clear. It ran from a wide stream, plunging between the shoulders of two rocks, all movement ceasing where it broke over the edge, falling calm and silent into the deep pool below. All of us boys swam except for Needham, who announced at breakfast that he had forgotten to bring his swimming trunks, and when we arrived at the swimming hole Mr. Persian told us all to go ahead, he would sit with Needham and keep him company and watch. We all dived in, and for an hour or more, I forgot them.

When it was too cold to swim anymore, I began to think about getting out, and looked up to settle on a route up across the rocks. I saw then that Mr. Persian was holding up the white jawbone of a sheep. He seemed to be explaining its intricacies to Needham, who sat with his white legs dangling over the lip of the rock and looked on, apparently fascinated. Mr. Persian must have found some joke to make about the sheep's teeth then, because the two of them laughed. In the warmth of the after-noon Mr. Persian's face had grown red and shining. A long piece of his hair had worked itself loose from his oiled scalp and flopped about like an ear of corn.

A scout is observant.

In the largest of the four tents, I slept next to Needham.

Every night, I saw him open his case and take out the little green hand towel I'd seen drooping over the side of his low yel-low bathtub at home. I saw him shut the case, then lock it with a small flat key, just like the one I'd imagined he would have. There was something ceremonial about the way he did it. This grubby boy who looked as though he hardly ever washed seemed to make a point of coming along when any of us went down to the stream at the bottom of the field to wash last thing in the freezing water. It was almost boastful, the way he hung his green rag around his neck those nights. He was always the last back afterwards. I used to lie in the dark listening to the click of his key in the lock of his suitcase, the rustle of his clothes as he removed them, his soft gasp as he slid down inside his cold nylon sleeping bag. One of his hands reached then behind his back, pulling the edge of his blue sleeping bag higher up over his shoulders, but I could still see, in the dark, the gleam of his white skin. I could see that he slept naked.

I thought about all the things we were supposed to have in our bags, all the items of clothing we were supposed to possess and to bring with us from our homes—pyjamas and spare shorts and shirts and handkerchiefs and bathing trunks—all the things on the list that Mr. Persian had given to us, copied out in his square script from page seventy-two of the handbook . I thought of the afternoon I'd gone into the little flat with its fishpaste smell and how much Needham had wanted me not to be there; of the happy look on his face as he'd sat by the path with Mr. Persian, cramming bright raspberries into his mouth with his bread and butter. I thought of his shrunken granny in her pasty dressing gown with the man's tie.

It is all a long time ago now and these days I wonder if his grandmother knew he had taken her old red suitcase, if she even knew he was with us.

These days when I think of the list on page seventy-two of the handbook, I find it almost unbearably sad.

It was the rain, on the last day, that set things going.

Mr. Persian woke us early so that we could do our climb in good time to pack up ready for the coach to take us home. We made breakfast and Mr. Persian set off to walk to the phone box to telephone the coach company to confirm the time of our departure.

The sky was white and blank and there was no sun. A damp vapour had drifted down from the peaks during the night, stealing its way into our tents and in between our clothes and our skin. By seven the mist had thickened, collapsing slowly into a steady drizzle and everyone went back into the tents for more clothes.

Only Needham stayed outside, eating his bread slowly. After five minutes he was soaked through, water dripped from the hem of his shorts into the hollow pockets between his feet and his black plimsoles. His shaven scalp looked blue, almost translucent, like the membrane of an egg. I could see the stubborn m-shaped line of his skull.

The rain had worked through his thin mac, his funny shirt clung to his narrow back. I could see the bumps on his spine. He'd got his old look back, his old stare, sullen and challenging.

He said then, to no one in particular, that he'd lost the key to his case and all his stuff was locked inside.

Qualtrone laughed, and I said, 'We believe you Needham.'

Then I went into the tent and brought out Needham's red case and set it down on the wet grass in front of everyone and slid the blade of my knife into the space between the metal catch and the lock. Needham looked very small and alone without Mr. Persian there to look after him. Still, I expected him to jump at me and make a grab for the knife, but he didn't speak or move, he stared at the ground, shivering in his sodden clothes. I wondered what he'd done with the key, if he'd thrown it in the fire, or into the stream at the bottom of the field. Under his shirt the hard point of his sternum stuck out like an apricot stone. He seemed frozen, and only stood there, a muscle beating very quick in his cheek.

The lid sprang open with a soft sigh.

There was no mirror and no ruched pocket, but the lining was shiny and red as I'd imagined it. The little green towel lay slumped all by itself in the middle, like a small square of thin wrinkled turf.

I told you, I'd never liked Needham. I'd never liked him at all.

Homecoming, 1909

She was the first woman I saw when we came into port and I knew at once that I was lost.

For a long time all I could do was stare, gripping the rail and wondering if, after all we'd heard, she could possibly be a dream. Some kind of wicked mirage.

She was tall, a large crimson hat slantwise on her head.

But it wasn't that—it wasn't her being tall, and it wasn't the hat. It was the rest of her, the rest of her in her leaf-green dress, looking like nothing I'd ever seen before. Such a comfortable, unrestrained softness in the look of her body, such a loose, easy look—it turned my tongue fat and dry in my mouth, my knees to water.

I thought of Cass, waiting for me in the narrow doorway of our house, the children all clustered around her. Becky, with her sweet smile, reaching up with her little hands and asking me, what presents have I brought?

A cream sash clasped the woman just beneath her breasts; from there the green cloth flowed down in a slender waterfall, a few supple folds; pooled in a narrow circle around her feet, and when she began to stroll along the quayside on the arm of the smart straw-boatered gentleman who accompanied her, I could see the slow, comfortable sway of her waist. I could see the gentle curve of her long back; the softly rounded flare of her hips. I groaned aloud. I bit my lip and began to moan and beat the rail with my fists.

Behind me the crew had begun to gather with their sunburned faces and raggy beards, with their foul breath and their rotting teeth still loose in their spongy gums. Jostling to get a look at the woman in the leaf-green dress and at all the others like her—because there were more, lots more, walking past our poor worn-out vessel on their way to meet the passenger steamer. A whole sea of them, in reds and blues and greys and yellows. All with that same free, easy look.

Next to me, Mr. Mingus, the third mate, pressed a grimy kerchief to his broken lips. Two of the boatsteerers sank down onto the deck. The rest continued to look, spellbound and speechless. Poor goggle-eyed buggers. A whole crowd of Rip Van Winkles, gaping at the world to which we had returned. The women different, not the way we'd left them. Not the way we'd banked on them being when we came back.

Thirteen months of ice and wind and narrow frozen hammocks since we last saw them. Thirteen months of hard bread and salt meat and oatmeal since we saw them as they used to be.

In the hold, our precious cargo. Chased and harpooned and hauled up out of the icy waters. What we wanted, hacked out from inside the giant mouth, separated from the greasy blubbery flesh. Scraped and cleaned and dried. Over and over. A year's work. Eighteen thousand pounds of whalebone. £25,000 at last year's prices.

Now this. The nightmare rumours from the other ships—all true.

Not one single woman in a corset.

De-boned, all of them.

'Mr. Mingus,' I said, turning away from the rail and laying my hand upon his shoulder.

'We are lost.'

Historia Calamitatum Mearum

My name is Patricia Singleton and I am the Latin teacher. By tomorrow, *I will have been* the Latin teacher. After that, it will be a case of *I was* the Latin teacher. Lately, I have come to think of my pathway to the scrapheap, my losing battle against Peter Tracey, as a series of inevitably changing verbs. *Ego sum. Ego fuero. Ego eram.* I am. I will have been. I was. There was a time when I had ten sets of twenty-five girls each, but this year there is only Jenny, and after Jenny, there will be no one.

I am packing.

I have packed all of Catullus, all of Livy, my complete *De Bello Gallico*. I have packed the photograph taken on our last trip to Rome. There I am in front of the Coliseum, third from the left, in the floppy straw hat and striped shirt-waist dress. It was taken in the spring of '96 (the year Peter Tracey arrived here) since when the trips have ceased to be viable, and our little group (five girls, and me) is testimony to my complete failure to maintain the popularity of Latin in this school, to convince the girls, and the governors, and the senior management, that the continuing study of a dead and ancient language is of some value.

Until the early nineties, it was compulsory here up until the third form. Since then, the girls have been voting with their feet, deserting the subject in droves. It hasn't helped matters that we are now what is called a *Technology College*, which brings with it from the government the indispensable sum of £100,000 a year, the *quid pro quo* being that every girl must now spend two hours a week doing technology with Peter Tracey.

God knows I've tried.

I have argued myself hoarse in front of the Head and the board of governors, my throat is raw from pleading with them to keep Latin as an option. I have practically killed myself (literally, in the case of the toga episode) over the last few years in my efforts to make the subject *fun* and *relevant*.

I have done everything I can think of to entice the girls back. I have held lunch-time sessions on Roman sex, after school Roman cookery clubs. I have told them about Elagabalus, the Emperor who had a secret life as a transvestite hooker, I have told them about the stripper Theodora, who did unspeakable things with geese in public places. I have given them recipes for dormice rolled in honey, for rose hip and calf brain custard, tips on the preparation of peacock and crane. We have cooked and eaten in the dining hall an authentic dish of sole with eggs.

With Siberian winds blowing in under every door, I have worn a toga with no tights in February, only a pair of thin-heeled flip flops between my bare feet and the freezing school lino, leaving me with the mother of all colds until well into April.

We have done Latin shopping lists, Latin letters to Father Christmas.

I have even stooped to a sort of parlour game where I invite the girls to throw at me any word or phrase in English that comes into their heads for me to translate into Latin. For example:

Gag me with a spoon. *Fac me cocleario vomere.*

My Jacuzzi is filled with Perrier. *Meum balineum calidum verticosum cum aqua scintillante fontana Gallica impletum est.*

Of all the ruses I've tried, this last one has been the most popular, but it is the one that leaves me feeling most upset, most depressed. I end up feeling like a performing monkey, a dancing bear.

One day after one such session, Jenny came up to me at the end. Bless her, I think she finds it quite painful to see me scraping the barrel in this way.

'*Summergimurne*, Miss Singleton?' she asked. Are we sinking?

'*Ita vero, summergimur*,' I said. Yes, we are sinking.

None of it has done any good, and this last year, as I've said, there has been only Jenny, and next year, there will be no one.

I have begun to think, Perhaps I am wrong? Perhaps it *is* more important to know how to make a flashing LED nightlight than to read Manilius on the Vault of Heaven, or to discover that Salmacis and Hermaphroditus are each one half of a seamless whole. Perhaps it is more deeply satisfying to shape and file a piece of blue acrylic into a name plate for one's desk than it is to unpick the ending from the beginning of a single word and unravel its meaning. Perhaps I have clung on too long to the wreckage. Perhaps they are right and I am wrong, perhaps it is a useless, impractical language and there are no circumstances left in which you would ever need it.

Perhaps.

Three weeks ago, I bumped into Peter Tracey outside the staff room.

I was standing close to the wall in the small space between the staffroom door and the mineral water dispensing machine.

'Patricia,' he said.

I jumped when he spoke my name, the shock struck me like a physical blow. It is so long since the two of us have exchanged even one word. We have settled over the years, while his star has risen and mine has fallen, into what most people here think of as a kind of silent truce.

Peter Tracey is tall and handsome, he wears quite good shirts in a range of pastel colours. He has brown curly hair and a strong prominent nose (which I can only describe as Roman). I would guess he is roughly half my age. He is generally adored, he is thought to be a very fun teacher.

'Patricia,' he said, touching his mouth with one of his large, practical hands, as people do when they are about to deliver some unpleasant news, and informed me that he'd been told by the Head that his department would be taking over the last remaining Latin room (my room, where I have been teaching Jenny) from the following Monday, and that I would be given the use of the vacant storeroom in the art block for my few remaining classes.

I tried to accept this piece of news with dignity, but I am no Marie Antoinette, and I found it impossible to withstand this final death blow, inevitable as it was, without bursting into tears.

Tracey blushed slightly and looked at his feet. Perhaps men like Peter Tracey are too young to carry a handkerchief. Anyway, he didn't offer me one, he just sort of sauntered off and away through the double doors at the end of the corridor.

I couldn't sleep that night, nor for several nights after that. I felt so crushed after what had happened in the corridor. The night before I was due to move into the store cupboard I lay awake until four, when I finally got up and wrote Peter Tracey a note.

I used a sheet of my best writing paper—laid, cream, A5— and wrote the message neatly in ink, folded it into quarters and wrote his initals, PJT, on the front.

*Vae, da mihi veniam vitae,*I wrote. Well, pardon me for living. And felt a little better.

When I arrived at school, I popped it into his pigeon hole before beginning the task of moving my things from my old room into my little cubby in the artblock.

My next note, the following day, took a slightly more assertive tone.

Potes currere, sed te occulere non potes.

I liked this one much more than the first: You can run, but you can't hide. I liked its symmetry, its edgy concision.

That afternoon Jenny had her last ever lesson with me before the start of her exams. I felt thoroughly miserable. When she'd gone, I spent an hour or so reading and then I collected my things—my cardigan, my mug and my briefcase—and turned off the storeroom light. It was long past the end of the day, and already the school appeared to be virtually deserted.

I crossed over into the main building to return my mug to the staffroom, and as I walked out through the darkening corridor on the ground floor, I saw a light on in the library. I paused, and saw Peter Tracey emerging from behind the bookcase where the dictionaries are kept. He sat down with the small Cassell's *Latin-English English-Latin* with the purple cover. I saw him take out my two pieces of paper, watched as he scrunched his handsome face into a frown of concentration, as he licked the tips of his fingers and began to leaf through the pages of the Cassell's.

He sat for about an hour, alternately staring at the notes and hunting through the purple dictionary. Then he slammed the Cassell's shut, snatched my notes from the table and began striding towards the doors.

I scuttled away.

Over the past two weeks, I have increased the frequency of the notes to two a day. The first I leave in the morning, after assembly, the second just before lunch. I've also begun to vary the messages, both in tone and in length. A few have been quite long, as apart from my packing, there has really been nothing left for me to do, but on the whole I have preferred to keep them quite brief, no more than a single line.

Every day, after school, long after the cleaners have gone and left behind their sweet refreshing perfumes of polish and ammonia, Peter Tracey has been staying on in the library, poring over my notes, of which there are (as of yesterday) thirty-two.

From time to time during the day, I leave my store room to go and look at him through the door of my old teaching room. He looks tired and wan. The other morning I saw him snap at one of the girls, which is most unlike him.

Now, I am packing. Tomorrow, I will have been the Latin teacher.

The only objects left in here are my briefcase, my cardigan, my mug, two flat empty boxes (which have turned out to be surplus to requirements), a half-used roll of brown tape, a pair of yellow-handled scissors.

There is also my five volume set of Manilius, which I can't quite bring myself to pick up off the shelf, it seems to me that when I pack away my Manilius, it will be the end of everything, I will have lost.

I left this morning's note in Peter Tracey's pigeon hole about an hour ago. I kept it short and to the point.

Homines tui similes pro ientaculo mihi appositi sunt. I eat people like you for breakfast.

Peter Tracey doesn't knock. He pushes open the door and for a moment he just stands there.

His appearance is disheveled, there is a bright sheen on his upper lip, a twitch tugging at the skin over his right temple. As he comes towards me, he seems to fill my little room completely.

His narrow, good-looking face is very close to mine now, I can see the veins in his handsome brown eyes. He grips my shoulders, my silence seems to produce in him an almost animal rage. He is shouting now,—*screaming*, I would say—I can feel his furious breath on my tightly sealed lips.

'Fucking tell me!' he bellows, 'Tell me what they fucking say!'

Metamorphosis

Telling me the news about Alice last week in the library, Arthur was rude to me for the first time ever.

Arthur who is never rude, who never has an unkind word to say to anyone. Arthur who in all the years we worked together was never anything but the most perfectly courteous old-fashioned gentleman.

He told me that Alice is pregnant, due in April, and then he said I should stop all this nonsense with the bird books, the videos. That everyone at the library knows it is just a pretext so I can come in and try to speak to Alice or say something abusive to Meakin. He said I am making Alice's life a misery and if I really cared about her I would stay away.

'But I am interested in birds, Arthur,' I said.

I wanted to explain to him that my bird research is a good thing. It is an occupation. I enjoy it and it takes my mind of Alice and Meakin for quite long periods during the day. It gives me a sense of purpose and usefulness.

But when I began to speak Arthur put his finger to his lips and said, 'Quiet now, Howard. This is a library,' as if he thought I might be about to start shouting.

He date-stamped my video and my book, looking with distaste at the photograph beneath its protective plastic cover: an

African crowned eagle ripping open the stomach of a large vervet monkey.

I caught a brief glimpse of Alice, talking to Gail over by the hessian-covered screens which divide the children's section from the rest of the library. I didn't think then that she looked particularly pregnant. She looked the same as always: tall, pale-ish skin, dark hair tied back in a pony-tail with a plain elastic band. It is worse though, her being pregnant. The thought makes me nauseous, ill. I'm really not sure I will be able to cope with Alice having Meakin's baby.

She flushed when she saw me and whispered something to Gail. Then she walked briskly away between the reading tables where the newspapers and periodicals are laid out, stepped into the store-room and closed the door. She always does that when I come into the library. She hides in the store-room until I have gone. Meakin I hardly ever seem to see. I think he hides from me too.

Philip Meakin is a strong, stocky man in his early thirties with short brown hair, no grey in it yet. How I hate him.

The best thing that has happened over the last few weeks has been my coming across the video, *The Flight of Eagles*. So far I have watched it twenty-three times. Useful as the books are, the video represents, I think, something of a breakthrough.

I used to work at the library, with Arthur and Gail and Alice and Philip Meakin, but when Alice and Meakin got married I found I couldn't stay.

My interest in birds—my *need* of them, if you like—began when I left.

I didn't resign in any formal way because until the moment I walked out I hadn't planned to go. I was standing at the front desk with Arthur. I must have been crying because Arthur looked so appalled. His small pale eyes were wide with sympathy but, being Arthur, he was shocked I suppose by my complete collapse, my total loss of control.

'I think I'm going to have to leave, Arthur,' I said and picked up my things—my green corduroy jacket draped over the back of the chair there, my newspaper and my bag.

The bird book was in my bag. I had put it there because the spine was badly broken and I had planned to mend it slowly at home, a few pages every evening.

It was the middle of the morning, a strange time to be at home in my kitchen. I opened the battered little book and began reading. The reading calmed me, and it was interesting. All of it. It was new to me and I found it quite absorbing. I had lived for forty-eight years and could only identify perhaps half a dozen common birds—magpie, pigeon, crow, robin, a few more maybe. I would not have been able to identify with any certainty a thrush or a swift or a lark or a nightingale, let alone anything more unusual, a buzzard, say, or a cormorant.

I discovered some interesting things:

That the wandering albatross possesses a special locking device which fixes its giant wings in position, allowing it to float above the ocean for weeks and months on end without touching land. That a flamingo will lose its pink colour if it doesn't eat enough brine shrimp and algae. That when a male bower bird (a small, plain brown thing) is ready to mate, it constructs a palatial hide-away beneath a canopy of orchid twigs, decorating the ground with pink blossoms and bright leaves, bits of broken glass and plastic and the shiny black carapaces of dead beetles.

Over the course of the following week I carefully repaired the book, pausing frequently to read anything that caught my attention.

The nictating membrane is a useful third eye-lid which protects against dust and light and water. In man, this membrane exists as a vestigial presence in the form of the tear duct.

The rich oil with which most birds anoint their feathers is secreted near the tail in the *preen gland*. Hence, preening.

A diving peregrine moves at a speed of 200 mph, the fastest creature on earth.

I returned to the library after an absence of about a week, having finished the book. I took out a few more, Gail saying as she checked them out that she hoped I was doing all right, that everything was okay.

I said, yes, I was okay really, not too bad.

On the whole though I have not done very well since being at home without working, without Alice. I have let things go rather, I sleep too much and eat poorly. I have begun to wake in the mornings with shooting pains in my face from clenching my teeth all night. I have stopped doing any laundry or going to the dry cleaners as there is no real reason for me to look smart. Now that nearly all my clothes are used up, I have hauled down the old ones bagged up on top of the wardrobe and have begun wearing them instead: T-shirts with writing on them, a thick cotton track-suit, the brown three-piece suit I wore at my graduation, an old parka.

These days I go to the library from time to time for more bird books; most days, I suppose. Alice is there of course. Alice is always there when I go in for the bird books. I always see her for a few moments before she spots me and goes off in the store-room because she thinks I am going to accost her. And Meakin—though I rarely see him—he's there somewhere in the library as well.

Most days Alice wears a cream dress with short sleeves and a round neck-line, a pair of fawn court shoes. She has taken his name but I still think of her as Alice Nolan.

The bird books are all together on the third wildlife shelf.

Somehow within the last week, in the seven days since Arthur told me the news, Alice has begun to look noticeably pregnant. She has started wearing loose dark trousers and various smock-like blouses. Her face is fuller, not so pale, her dark hair thick and glossy.

It is interesting that every single bird in existence, without exception, gives birth by laying eggs.

I had never really considered the reason for this, though it seems obvious to me now. It has to do with weight. Everything about a bird has to do with weight and buoyancy—its hollow bones, the extra air sacs in its body. If a female bird tried to fly around with her gestating young inside her body, she would drop out of the sky.

I usually wait a few moments before going into the library. In that short period of time before she sees me, while I stand outside and look in from the street through the glass of the main doors, Alice looks very happy.

When you come to be interested in something, it seems all of a sudden to be everywhere. I have found, for example, that there is almost always a story about birds in the newspaper these days.

A flamingo at the Chicago Zoo has been fitted with a wooden leg.

A storm-driven Little Auk has been found marooned on Blackpool Pleasure Beach. The bewildered creature is being kept in a cage in which a mirror has been installed, so that the poor thing will not think itself alone.

I even came across the following on the Letters Page of a free magazine I found lying around in the stairwell of my building:
Hope is the thing with feathers
That perches in the soul.

I have cut that out, and stuck it onto my shaving mirror.

The library's collection of bird books is patchy, slightly eccentric. There are forty-eight books all told, including a good dozen privately published pamphlets by local enthusiasts, and various field guides. My favourite books are those with the best photography—close-ups of a pink-skinned cuckoo hatchling sending the pale speckled egg of a reed warbler smashing to the ground. The communal nest of a group of sociable weavers, draped over a tree in the Kalahari like a vast shaggy rug.

There is a book I like called *The Language of Birds* which turns out to be a curious little miscellany of bird-related vocabulary.

The Hebrew for two-tone owl is *o-ah*. The following is a list of collective nouns: A parliament of owls. An exaltation of larks. A murmuration of starlings.

In my other reading I have learned that a male wild turkey with small neck wattles is unlikely to attack a male wild turkey with large neck wattles.

I have learned that collisions between birds and aircraft are surprisingly common and potentially catastrophic.

There are just three bird videos on the shelves at the library: *Wildfowl*, *The Behaviour of Penguins* and *The Flight of Eagles*. Finding *The Flight of Eagles* is the most exciting thing that has happened to me in the course of these miserable weeks. It is what gave me my idea.

I have been reading about eagles for some time now and I cannot imagine there is a living creature anywhere that would not be frightened if confronted by one. Bald, crowned, golden, harpy, short-toed—they are all different but they all have the same beady eyes and sloping beaks, they all possess, more or less, the same mean face, the same grand ambitions when it comes to the kill. The South American harpy will swoop into trees and pick off sloths the size of sheep dogs. The European short-toed eagle will attack a viper whole. And then there is—or rather was—Harpagornis, the largest eagle the world has ever seen. Now extinct, it preyed on the large flightless, ostrich-like moas of New Zealand. It had a nine-foot wingspan, talons as big as a tiger's claws. I imagine its spread shadow across the sun, the creak of its enormous wings, its terrifying speed. The hysterical moa, thundering through the forest. Harpagornis skewered to its soft back.

Yesterday I had another small altercation with Arthur. He said Alice had to go home early yesterday she was so upset.

'Why must you keep coming, Howard?' he said. He spoke in a harsh whisper, nothing like his ordinary gentle voice, and he looked so angry. Arthur who has been my friend and colleague for so long.

I tried to speak quietly too.

'My life is very empty without Alice, Arthur,' I said. 'Without my job. My research gives me a feeling of usefulness, of being still alive. I need to come to the library.'

Arthur folded his arms and looked me in the eye.

'So you don't come here to see Alice and Philip then.'

I have never known Arthur to be sarcastic before. I couldn't lie.

'Yes I do come to see Alice. And Meakin. I do. I can't help it, Arthur. But I also come for the birds.'

Arthur stood with his arms folded across his Fair Isle slipover. His little face had a cold, sceptical look which I found suddenly very irritating.

'I can't do nothing, Arthur.' Now I was shouting and the people over at the newspaper and periodicals table were looking at us. Gail's head appeared from behind one of her hessian screens. 'I can't just carry on as if nothing has happened to me,' I went on, and then I said, and I suppose I shouldn't have, 'We're different, Arthur, you and I. I'm not like you, Arthur.'

Arthur blinked and drew in his neck like a tortoise.

Arthur has his own love story.

It happened a few years ago: a girl who came to the library for a while, looking for information about the local hatting industry in the nineteenth century. She was not pretty and she always came in alone and perhaps those two things together were what made Arthur think he would succeed. Or perhaps he simply believed after a time—after helping her every day over all those weeks—that he had become important, even indispensable, to her. Anyway she stopped coming one day. She had finished her study I suppose and no longer needed to use the library, or Arthur, anymore.

Arthur never mentioned her afterwards. For a long time whenever the big oak and glass doors at the front of the building opened he would look up from whatever he was doing to see if it was her coming back. But he never tried to find her, he never went looking for her, he refused ever to talk about her and he made no attempt to fill the hole she had left in his life. He remained quiet and self-contained. He carried out all his duties with the same brisk efficiency as before. He still came out with me at lunch-time to buy a sandwich from the shop across the road. He had the same sandwich he'd always had, egg mayonnaise with chopped onion. He wore the same pair of brown trousers, the same green jumper with the short zip at the neck which he alternated with his two slipovers, the plain navy one, and the one with a Fair Isle design on a chestnut background.

'Talk to me, Arthur,' I'd say from time to time and he knew exactly what I meant but he always ignored me and would straightaway start up a conversation about something else entirely.

He disapproves of my behaviour now, I can see that, I can understand it. But I have always believed that he would feel better if he could find some outlet for his misery.

'I do come for the birds, Arthur,' I said now, as gently as I could, trying to patch things up. 'Not just for them, it's true, but I do come for them too.'

Arthur said nothing. He pursed his lips and date-stamped my books. He charged me 30p for the microfilm copies I'd made that day of various aeroplane accidents reported in the newspapers, and renewed *The Flight of Eagles*.

A big-ish eagle beats its wings twenty-four times a minute.

I practise mostly in the evenings, using the kitchen clock.

I have had only one reply to my letters, from Manchester. It was very short; the tone was lofty and sarcastic and full of scorn and I have thrown it away. No one else has replied.

No one else has replied so today I am going to go anyway and make the attempt.

For a big part of the journey from Euston, I don't think about Alice once. I think only about what I'm going to be doing when I arrive. I practise my breathing, the slow counting. I feel light, optimistic, excited. I don't think of Alice at all except once when we stop at Acton Town. Outside on the platform, through the scratched window glass of the train I see a strong, stocky man in a dark suit holding a child in a blue duffel coat by the hand.

Meakin.

My breathing buckles, my counting stops. No, not Meakin. Of course not Meakin. Meakin is miles and miles away in the library with Alice and Arthur and Gail. I take several long breaths and begin counting again, and continue for the remainder of the journey.

I have mentioned the accidents.

I first came across them about three weeks ago. Two of them, only a few days apart, one reported in *The Times*, the other in *The Telegraph*. The first involved a Lockheed Electra which took off from Boston airport and collided with a flock of starlings. All sixty-two people on board died in the crash. In the second, a Vickers Viscount struck a flock of whistling swans over Glasgow airport. The plane went into an uncontrolled dive, all seventeen people on board perished.

I found more cases on the library's microfilm, going back over the last five years, involving woodpigeons and oystercatchers, rooks, Canada geese, gulls. Take-off and landing are the most dangerous times.

The accidents trouble me, I can't stop thinking about them. I dream about them. The torn metal and broken beaks and drifting feathers and human corpses falling out of the sky.

I have never flown.

I have never set foot, even, in an airport terminal, let alone on the glittering tarmac of the runway.

There is a section of the outer fence made of wire, a temporary barrier adjacent to some building work. Pretty soon I have made a man-hole sized opening and climb through.

The airport is vast. Unbelievably noisy. I hadn't counted on it being so noisy and busy and big. As far as my eye can see the flat ground is dotted all over with aircraft, either about to take off, or just having landed. I position myself about a hundred yards from the end of the nearest runway. After a while, the starlings come, moving in quick, skittery patches across the sky: a murmuration of starlings. If they are making any sound, I can't hear it. The only noises are the screams of the planes overhead, the rumble of the nearest plane waiting to move—a huge, barrel-chested Lufthansa monster.

I close my eyes to shut out the noise of the planes; to concentrate fully on what I am doing. Very slowly, rhythmically, I begin flapping my arms and counting. One potato, two potato. Very slow: po-ta-to. I have practised this at home a thousand times, with and without the video. When I count, and flap my arms, it gives exactly the right number of wing beats per minute. Twenty-four. The same as an eagle. Twenty-four mean menacing wingbeats. Eighteen potato. Nineteen. Inside the sleeves of my parka my arms feel heavy and there's a slow burn starting at the top where they are pinioned to the rest of my body. The whole thing is both exhausting and soothing, calming and at the same time extremely exciting. High up the starlings swoop and dive, very nervy, more like a shoal of fish or a swarm of bees, a dark panicky mass. And now they see me, these birds, or one of them does and the rest follow. Or they have somehow sensed the danger I present, and by whatever strange communal intelligence it is that governs their behaviour, they all make one last dive, change shape again, rise up and are gone. The plane lifts itself safely into the clear, open sky.

I shake my head and chuckle, and experience—for the first time in months—a profound sense of calm; of thorough and complete satisfaction, of something close to contentment. All around me, now that the plane and the birds have gone, the busy airport seems suddenly silent—lulled—and I stand there, grinning; wrapped in the quiet celebration of the moment. If there are loud noises I don't hear them. The only sound is behind me somewhere, a dull, remote kind of thrumming I cannot immediately identify.

Only when I turn do I see the long line of men in luminous yellow jackets, fanning out across the runway, jogging towards me, the thunderous tattoo of their heavy boots on the tarmac becoming steadily louder and more furious.

There are perhaps a dozen of them and they all look very stern; a few of them start swearing at me when they are still some distance away, one of them refers to me loudly as *the prick in the parka*. They have no interest at all in what I try to tell them about the success of my experiment. I am seized, roughly handled, frog-marched, half-dragged back to the terminal. Arrested.

And the strange thing is, that amid the clamour and the shouting and the gruff commands and the painful snapping-on of the handcuffs, all I can think of is Arthur. Arthur with his pale blinking eyes and his broken heart; Arthur with his delicate brand of silent restraint, his decorum, his sweet quiet dignity. Arthur who has been my friend for twenty years, who over the past few months has come to think the worst of me. And as the police van begins to speed away from the airport, I find myself wondering what Arthur will say when I tell him about this afternoon—if he will purse his lips and click his tongue with irritation and disbelief and carry on stamping his books as if he wants nothing more to do with me. Or if, in fact, he will look up at me with a weary sigh, and give his head a small indulgent shake, and suggest a sandwich.

In Skokie

Good, I thought, when the horrible old thing disappeared.

No more having to watch it come creeping up the street, low-slung and close to the ground, slow and heavy and brown, eighteen foot nose to tail like some gigantic salt-water crocodile; Myron's hat just visible above the steering wheel.

Myron was beside himself, you should have seen him.

For weeks he went round distributing flyers and taping up posters, the way people do when they have lost a cat or a child. Sometimes he'd just stand and stare at the empty driveway. He couldn't believe what the police said, that they had no leads, that all they could do was make out their report and let us know if it turned up.

These days he's much better. He's been going through the automobile classifieds circling anything he likes the sound of. There's a dark blue Buick station wagon he fancies, a cream Oldsmobile saloon. He's stopped going out with his flyers, his posters; when he comes in at five-thirty he eats his dinner and then he goes to the den and turns on the TV and after a half-hour he's asleep. He's like the old Myron again.

Me, I just can't seem to settle. I keep thinking about that old Chevrolet, slouching down the street, past Walgreens, past Dunkin' Donuts. Rolling west across the desert, taking in the sights: Mesa Verde, the Hoover Dam, Vegas. Nosing north maybe, across the border, into the cool air of the Rockies.

Myron's car, making a break for it.

The Visitors

They were both smaller than I'd expected, especially Mr. Dickens, though I suppose all men are puny compared with Dr. de Vitre. He towered above them, pumping their hands, smiling and sweating and already babbling away in a stream of excited chatter. He waved them into his study and they went in, Reverend Danby following. Through the partly open door, I saw the Gillow cabinet in the corner where the doctor keeps the instruments of coercion. Also, on the mantlepiece, the hateful little clock, brown and humpbacked, that chimes the hour with a clear, ringing sweetness, like the notes struck on a glass by a silver fork.

Afterwards, I cut out the report of the visit from the newspaper, and pasted it into the visitors' book:

'Mr. Charles Dickens with his friend the artist Mr. Wilkie Collins after a tour of the Lake District arrived from Carlisle last Saturday at the King's Arms Hotel. On Sunday, the two gentlemen, accompanied by the Reverend F.B. Danby, visited the Asylum and were shown its principal departments and made many enquiries as to its management. On the following day the two gentlemen left for Doncaster.'

It is of course rather incomplete. It does not mention, for instance, that the cook at the King's Arms was blubbing half of

Sunday night because Mr. Dickens sent his entire dinner back to the kitchen untouched—tongue, chops, lemon pudding, everything. It seems his visit here took away his appetite.

I'd thought perhaps some of us might have been introduced when they arrived, that the doctor might have organised some sort of welcoming party in the hall before beginning his tour of the facilities. Myself and some of the other nurses and female attendants perhaps, but we were not asked, and after I'd watched the men withdraw, I took myself off upstairs, it being early and the women being still locked in their dormitories.

The quiet up in the galleries and bedrooms is remarkable here, and that morning when I went up everything was as peaceful as ever. Only the soft, intermittent hooting from Ruby punctuated the quiet, and the whisper of Edith's nails on the floorboards.

I went in as usual to check on Violet Bowl, who had at that time been with us for a little less than a month. She had arrived one dreary Monday morning, without her wits, without a name, and, it seemed then, without a voice. It was I who first called her Violet, on account of the fine, branching veins that come creeping out from her spine, just beneath the white skin at the back of her neck. They are dark and purplish and I looked at them while I washed her for the first time in the bath, and again when I buttoned her into a clean gown. The rest of her is so pale and clear, the veins are very striking. I said to her, 'I will call you Violet.' She has never objected and that is what she has become.

Her other name, that of Bowl, derives from a strange incident in the dining hall a few days afterwards.

I have always liked the dining hall best of all our rooms here, with its tall palms and all the tables laid out so neat and everything in such perfect order. It is quite a sight in the evening to see all the women here in their chairs, sipping their coffee and eating their bread and butter, everything so tranquil and cheerful. There is of course the occasional scene, outbursts of noise and excitement, and sometimes worse, usually from Charlotte Gittings, who is a creature of persistently filthy habits. But for the most part, I can think of no more restful place on earth.

Violet sat silently, taking neat bites out of her bread and drinking from her cup. She looked up and down the rows of other women but seemed to find nothing of any interest until on this particular evening her eyes fell upon a large bowl in the centre of the table. She became agitated and began smoothing her hair in an urgent, panic-stricken fashion. She rose from her chair and before I could stop her, she reached forward and picked up the bowl and placed it very carefully on her head, in the manner of a crown, or a hat, or some other kind of headpiece. I was about to go to her when Dr. de Vitre entered the hall. He saw our new arrival at once, standing in front of her chair wearing the bowl on her head. He approached swiftly from the far end of the hall, growing steadily larger in his flapping black coat as he came lumbering towards us. Violet smiled at him as he came near her. She has a very sweet, expectant smile.

She was still smiling at him when he put his hand gently on her arm.

The doctor is at all times very gentle and kind with the women. We are all under strict instructions to behave with the utmost kindness towards them. 'Love,' he is fond of saying, 'is a great improver of the idiot.'

Dr. de Vitre is not like other men. He is kind and gentle and devoted to the women here and I know he will never leave us.

For a brief moment, the two of them stood smiling at each other, Violet and the doctor, his huge hand resting on her arm and her looking up at him with her lips parted in that hopeful smile. But when he made to remove the object from her head, she jerked away from him and the bowl clattered onto the table and from there onto the wooden floor where it broke into a thousand glittering pieces. She flew at him then like a cat and bit his hand, on the soft fleshy part below the thumb. Sucking at his wound, he said to me between his teeth, 'Take her upstairs. Stay with her. Do not leave her until she is calm.'

I stayed with her all night. First I coaxed her into a nightgown, and then I brushed her hair for a long time, over and over, which seemed to soothe her. Eventually she slept and I watched her till dawn from my chair, wondering if she suffered in her sleep, if her dreams were mad.

The doctor has a great interest in the dreams of the poor creatures here. Sometimes I can hear him prowling about in the galleries in the dark, as if his patients will reveal to him out of their
sleep the obscure sources of their lunacy.

Once I heard Dr. Smail, our visiting surgeon, express the
belief that our miserable weather is partly to blame, that
women are particularly susceptible to the melancholy effects of
the rain. Dr. de Vitre laughed uproariously at this suggestion,
causing the visiting surgeon to blush. 'If that were the case,
Smail, the entire female population of Lancashire would be as
mad as hatters. Every single one. Mad as a hatter.'

The day after the bowl incident I went upstairs as usual shortly
after half past eight in the morning to check that the women
were clean and dressed in their bedrooms before being taken off
to the needlework room. I decided to go to Violet last, and to
spend a little time sitting with her, perhaps brushing her hair.
When I unlocked the door, I did not see her at first. There was
Edith, trying to dig one of her holes by the window. Violet's
gown lay across her bed, torn from top to bottom. Then I saw her
in the corner, and then the door to Dr. de Vitre's study must
have opened, because as I stood in the doorway looking at Violet
Bowl, the horrible brown clock on the mantlepiece down there
began to strike the hours.

Seven, eight, nine. The same bright note as that other clock.
A sudden heat in my throat, a sharp freezing below my heart.
The end of time. I closed my eyes against the silvery chimes of
the clock, and the sight of Violet Bowl.

I woke on the leather couch in Dr. de Vitre's study and saw the
shape of his dark back at his desk. He turned. I raised myself but
he put out his hand. He told me to rest. He said the sitting up all
night with Violet Bowl had made me ill.

I lay there for a while. I'd never seen the Gillow cabinet up
close before, with all the old means of restraint inside, a kind of
private museum the doctor shows to our many visitors, the cuffs

and leg braces and cunningly made jackets all there behind the glass. There are little bottles too, Dr. Hunter's green insane powders, and his patent Brazil salts.

I stared out of the window at the vast white sky, the sweep of the path, the gardens, the dark bulk of the cedars. Off to the side, the beginning of the greenhouses, the cemetery beyond. The doctor is very proud of the grounds, and rightly so. We have made considerable progress in cultivating, planting, and laying out the rough moorland surrounding us.

He continued to write for a while at his desk, and then he brought me some tea.

I asked him if he thought Violet might have a chance of recovery.

He is reluctant, these days, to talk of effecting a cure. He seems to think lunacy an illness that can never be cured in the manner of some bodily sickness. But he is always hopeful of what he calls recovery, by which he means being able to leave this place and resume a life outside.

'Well?' I said.

He pushed out his lips and drew one of his big hands across the back of his neck and then, as always, replied in a stream of rapid, repeated words. 'I think she has been too long, too long in the same condition. Early intervention is the key. Early intervention. That is the secret. In Violet's case I believe there has been a festering.'

I finished my tea and he asked me if I felt better.

'Yes. A little. Thank you.' I said.

There was a silence between us. He is a good man, the doctor. He is wedded to this place. He says he will never leave it. I have heard him tell Dr. Smail. He says the only way he will leave it will be 'in a box'.

'What happened?' he asked gently, the same soft, urging way he speaks to his patients.

'She had taken off her clothes. Her bedsheet was torn and wound about her head in pieces. It hung down her back onto the floor.' He frowned.

'How did she seem to you?'

'Seem?' I said.

He leaned forward in his chair. I heard it creak beneath his weight. He nodded.

'Beautiful,' I said. 'Like a bride.'

The morning Mr. Dickens came with his friend Mr. Collins, Violet Bowl escaped. I do not know how it happened, but when I came upstairs following their arrival, the door to her bedroom was open. Edith was digging happily, Charlotte lay quietly on her bed, plucking at some invisible annoyance, but Violet was gone, and when I attempted to open the door to its full extent, I found I could not. There was some soft obstruction beneath the door and when I stooped to look I saw that it was Violet's torn nightgown.

I looked in all the bedrooms, in the needlework room, in the dining hall. I searched the kitchen, the laundry and the drying yard but she was nowhere to be found. I went into the garden and made my way down the path towards the cemetery. Dr. de Vitre and his party of visitors were approaching from the opposite direction, and there on the lawn, against the black trunk of one of the cedars, was Violet.

She was very, very pale, white and naked but for the thing she had contrived to cloak about her head and shoulders, a sort of drooping grey caul, the end of which trailed for several yards across the grass and lapped against the tree in a bundle of trapped leaves and twigs. It was, I could see then, a length of garden netting of the sort that hangs in some of the greenhouses to support the heavy fruit. The netting was glazed here and there with cobwebs, and in the light from the white sky, it shimmered.

She began to move towards the men. Dr. de Vitre stroked the back of his neck in the usual way but seemed unsure of what to do. He watched Violet with a kind of grave curiosity. Reverend Danby stared at his shoes and Mr. Collins seemed to struggle with the suppression of a lecherous smirk. Mr. Dickens also seemed rather taken with her, and was smiling when she came up to him, very close, and touched his beard and called him Albert. He continued to smile at her, though rather nervously, and she, more confidently, smiled back. He looked sideways at Dr. de Vitre who merely raised his heavy chin with a nod of assent. Mr. Dickens offered Violet his arm, and she took it. Her eyes did not leave his face. She looked as if she would cling to its promise for ever.

They all proceeded slowly back towards the main building, Dr. de Vitre in front with the Reverend Danby, then Violet on Mr. Dickens' arm, Mr. Collins bringing up the rear behind the swish of the garden netting. A ripe, peachy scent escaped, then died beneath the odour of rotting leaves. Mr. Dickens passed a few inches from me on the path. 'Be careful,' I whispered. 'If you leave her now, she will bite.'

He turned sharply and looked at me, haughty and at the same time bewildered, as if he took me for one of the patients out for a ramble in the damp grass of the grounds.

I followed them into the house and stood in the hallway, listening to the rustle of leaves and twigs on the wooden floor as they made their way up towards Violet's bedroom. I heard the doctor call to one of the attendants, a brief murmuring of voices as the gentlemen took their leave.

A loud, protesting squeal of pain.

In a little while, they all came downstairs. I did not move, only stood at the tall window in the hallway and watched the rapid drizzle moving in from the moor. I wasn't aware of Dr. de Vitre speaking when he first addressed me. When he spoke again, though, I knew it was for a second time and I heard like an echo the soft whispering sound of my own name.

'Miss Havisham,' he said. 'Our visitors are leaving now.'

I must have looked at Mr. Dickens with something like loathing then, for he could not keep my gaze, and turned away, nursing his bandaged hand. My throat hot and dry, I climbed the staircase, up towards the tranquility of the galleries, to where the lunatics are.

Ugly Sister

There had been an understanding between the two sisters that they would take it in turns.

They'd been doing it for a long time now, ever since they'd found themselves deserted by their husbands, simultaneously single again and living together in the white house up on the cliff above the town with Sylvia's little girl, Grace.

It seemed they'd always known who should be hanging back, who should be allowed to put herself forward. The first summer, there had been the American on the beach at St. David's. He'd been Sylvia's and Hazel had obliged by taking Grace off for an ice-cream and then for a walk all the way to the cathedral. After that there'd been Hazel's little adventure with the man on the bus after Christmas shopping in Cardiff. He'd been hers, there'd been no question. And then, most recently, there'd been the red-haired soap powder salesman one Saturday afternoon in Oxwich who'd been Sylvia's, but then hadn't, as it turned out. Sylvia had wanted him too much, that was the trouble, she'd been completely carried away and had frightened him off.

As children, as girls, they'd always shared possessions by taking it in turns with the better things. The red tricycle, the roller skates. Later, a particular pair of silvery Van Dal heels. Boys they'd never had to share in those days, there were always plenty around in the town and the two of them had been popular enough, attractive in a tall, lean way, and it was not at all surprising that marriage had come along and separated them for a time.

But now, somehow, their circumstances—living together in Sylvia's white house up on the cliff, marooned by their husbands—had seemed to make them into a pair, an oddity. It was as if there'd been the same problem with the two of them, something sisterly that had made the husbands go. Some defect which had particularly to do with them. The two sisters, living together, did not seem to invite the approach of men.

The episode with the soap powder salesman had been unfortunate. He had seemed so keen to begin with, had invited Sylvia to choose herself a present from the promotional samples in the boot of his car. She had picked out a Fairy Liquid apron and a pair of *Pure Honey* stockings, and Hazel had been all set to make herself scarce, to invent some errand she needed to do with Grace. But then he'd looked at his watch and said, well, he must be going now, that it had been nice to meet them, that he hoped Sylvia would enjoy wearing the apron and the stockings. Hazel knew that Sylvia had let her hopes get very high that time, that her sister thought something lasting might have resulted from the meeting. It was a shame for her that nothing had come of it, nothing at all.

Hazel had wondered how the next one would come to them, the next one, who would be hers. Every day, she was prepared, because there was always the possibility of something happening. She pummiced the flaky skin on her heels, Immacced her long, lean legs. Dressed herself carefully—black slacks and a close-fitting sweater in something soft, mohair or lambswool. By eight in the morning she was always softly powdered and sweetly perfumed.

And then he had come to them, the dark-haired stranger, the collector of wind-tolerant seaside plants, like a gift.

The sisters had finished preparing the house for Grace's birthday party. They were sitting together at the bay window looking down onto the road when they saw him coming towards them. Slowly in a black car, a map spread out across the steering wheel. Lost, clearly, and in need of assistance. Should Hazel go out to him? Put on her coat and position herself by the gate to help him when he passed? Hazel thought that she should. She turned in her chair, rose to go, and then she saw her sister.

Sylvia sat, lips parted, leaning forward, one hand gently patting and lifting the back of her hair where it curved under against her neck. Hazel felt the memory of the other one come creeping out of the wallpaper, the salesman who had never followed through with what he'd seemed to be offering. Hazel saw the set of her sister's jaw and knew that Sylvia had no intention of hanging back, that she would not be waiting her turn. Hazel had the feeling that this one had already been stolen from her.

When she looked back out through the window, the black car was parked at the gate. The day was warm, a light October breeze blew soft patterns across the grass in front. They had the door open, and with Hazel still gaping at her sister's lean, eager, thieving profile, he'd walked right into the hall and put his dark head round the door into the front room. Hazel caught the taste of him riding in on the warm air, something fresh and sharp, a garden smell.

She has never forgotten it. The stink of plants on his clothes and in his skin.

She could hardly say afterwards exactly how things had happened. How one minute the two of them were with him at the door, both speaking at once in their fight to be the one to give him directions to the nursery. How the next minute he was standing with his black shoes on the patterned rug in the dining room saying the gammon smelled nice. And then she and Sylvia had said, in embarrassing, precise unison, 'Do stay. Do stay and have something.' She'd felt her cheeks go hot, a scalding fury with Sylvia for making her look too eager by being so eager herself.

She was glad, at least, that everything looked so nice, that he had been brought to them on the day of the party.

A long trestle table stood against the far wall, opposite the bay window, covered in a white cloth lapping the patterned rug. Strawberries in a glass dish, pineapple chunks in mother's rose-coloured bowl. The warm gammon, sausages on sticks. Cheese and silver onions, a yellow jelly in a rabbit mould, shivering as if it were afraid.

Only Sylvia spoiled everything by hovering so close to the man when it was not her turn, smiling and arching her pencilled brows. Offering him tea in the little-girl voice she used for the men. The two sisters brought him over to the table together, like bodyguards, helped him to some warm gammon and a silver onion and urged him to try a mouthful of the yellow jelly.

He told them he was on a short holiday, staying at Bed & Breakfasts along the coast, buying the plants he was after wherever he could. He'd called ahead to the nursery here for the oleaster he wanted and they were keeping it for him, if only he could find the damn place. The three of them laughed together then, the sisters' voices clashing as they both began again with the directions.

He'd definitely been looking at her then though. Perhaps he'd sensed that she was more the gardener of the two of them. She saw herself leading him out into the back, into the garden that ran all the way down to the edge of the cliff. She saw herself describing how magnificent it would all be in the summer, with the bright flames of the kniphofia, the warm pleasing scent of the olearia. The soft clouds of blue and pink and white with the flax, tamarisk and daisy bush all in bloom. Sylvia could hardly even name them. She would be left standing, she'd have nothing to contribute, nothing with which to strike up a conversation.

Yes, he'd definitely been looking at her then. To this day, Hazel is sure of that. When he leaned forward to take up the frightened rabbit with his spoon, his dark hair almost touched her face and she'd caught again the sharp perfume in his clean dry cheeks. Briefly, then, she had the feeling that everything, after all, was as it should be. His mouth full, he'd smiled at her, gesturing with his spoon to show his appreciation of the food. Flecks of yellow rabbit clung to his teeth and he licked them away with his tongue. She pictured him, staying on for a night or two at the Bed & Breakfast down the road, the two of them sharing a few inches of Bristol Cream in the tooth mug there in the room. She tried a gentle, probing question, Would he be in the area for a while, after his visit to the nursery?

She remembers now that he hadn't seemed to hear her then, she remembers hating Sylvia for what she was doing. The rest of it has only become clear in the replaying of the scene, which visits her now like a nightmare.

The girls, Grace's friends, had begun to arrive, all in one big frilly clump, in their frothy pastel frocks and white ankle socks. He was leaning away from Hazel now, looking at all the girls who were jumping about watching Grace tear open her presents. That was when the fresh, green scent of his skin had got away from her, losing itself in the chatter of the noisy girls.

A thousand times she has asked herself if she could have prevented it. She has asked herself if the two of them had repelled him by their eagerness, by their both wanting him too much, falling over each other trying to get his attention, inviting him to more food, pressing him to stay.

She has asked herself if she could have prevented it by holding his interest herself, by being, perhaps, a little more beautiful.

When she'd come back into the room after fetching the cake from the kitchen, the cake with the thirteen candles on it, he was bending down and talking to Grace. She was showing him her presents. A box of Milk Tray. Some mittens and a packet of socks, a record in a white paper sleeve.

Grace smiled at the man. He was tall and dark and had a strange perfume like nothing she was used to inside the rooms of this house. It was like grass, mingled with something else too which was different from the cloying sweetness she was used to, the thickly scented skin of her mother and her aunt. It was like the nice smell of other girls' fathers.

To Hazel, it had seemed like more than a favour then, his offering to drive the girls home at the end of the party, saving them getting the car out of the garage. It had seemed like a promise, the next stage in their getting to know him, a kindness there would be some opportunity to repay. Each sister had felt a fierce certainty that she would be the one who would find that opportunity.

They'd watched him make room for the girls in the back, moving a box of plants, sea lavender and eryngium, into the boot, brushing off with his hand the grainy trail of sand and soil left behind on the leather. They watched him open the passenger door for Grace, who would show him the way. Each of the sisters was as full of hope at that moment as the other, in spite of the way he'd said, 'Goodbye then, ladies.' Neither of them had liked that. *Ladies*. The way it made a pair of them.

He hadn't stopped when he dropped Grace back afterwards. Hazel heard her niece's step in the hall, and when she looked out through the bay window, his black car had already moved away.

Hazel dreams that he'll come back to them one day. She is fairly sure that if he ever comes, she will kill him.

She has sat, often, in the bay window looking down onto the road and imagined him strolling along it, walking back towards them from the direction of the nursery, his purchases made, a flat box of plants in his arms. She has seen herself going out into the white garage attached to the house, slowly backing out into the road in Sylvia's green Austin, picking up speed quickly as she motors towards him. She's seen the shallow box twirl lazily in the air, yellow grasses and silvery shrubs like handfuls of feathers breaking out of their pots and floating down with the man. Shining leaves and crumbs of earth settling themselves over his dead, dry face, his dark fanned-out hair.

Hazel has begun to knit a blanket, a blue one because she feels in her bones that it will be a boy. She will wrap the baby up in it when he is born and keep him warm. She has come to think of the blanket as something powerful that will help him after his awful start. He will be safe and they will look after him. He will grow up and he will forgive them for everything and so, perhaps, will Grace.

She and Sylvia talked once, briefly, once it began to be clear what had occurred, of going to the police, but Sylvia wouldn't have it and in the end Hazel came round to her way of thinking. It was better to be quiet about everything. Grace, after all, has never, ever talked about what happened to her. No word about it, about the man, has ever been spoken.

What matters now is Grace, what's important is to protect her in every way, to make her life easy and comfortable.

When spring comes, they leave the white house and take a small one further down the coast.

It's Hazel who arranges everything, who finds the new house to rent, who notifies the school that they are moving out of the area.

'We've found the prettiest place,' she tells her niece. 'You won't need to go to school when we move. You can do your work at home for a change, your mother and I will teach you between us.'

It turns out that Hazel takes care of all the teaching, Sylvia scarcely seems up to it. Sylvia seems to shrink from any of the necessary arrangements. She has taken it all very, very hard. She is quiet and brooding, spends her days reading in her chair in the corner of the front room.

Hazel asks Grace if she minds moving house, if she'll miss her old school. The girl shrugs, says she'll miss her friends.

Everything Hazel does now, she does with Grace in mind, so that everything will go smoothly after the terrible thing that has happened.

Mostly they stay indoors, Sylvia reading in her chair, crumpled and withdrawn from everything. Hazel's life is taken up with caring for Grace, with her lessons, with cooking the things she likes to eat, with choosing books for her from the library.

Hazel goes out for all the shopping. In the street, she keeps her eyes down, the world seems to her these days to be full of men. She looks away from them, as if she's afraid of some fresh horror, some new ambush.

Sylvia does come out sometimes, to walk with Hazel and Grace in the early morning when the beaches are empty. Only a few times they have been met by other people, who gape rudely at the two women with the schoolgirl. Frail legs in white socks, a fair pony tail in a nylon band, damp and straggly in the salty wind, big and swollen like a sparrow. Hazel has watched their mouths fall open, blame spilling out onto the wet sand like fish, hanging around in heaps behind their backs after she's taken Grace by the hand and led her away, back into the little house behind the dunes.

Grace, mercifully, doesn't seem to notice people looking. Hazel is proud of her, of the girl's quiet strength. Hazel has read the postcards her niece sends to her old friends. They're full of ordinary things, about the new house, about the weather and ice-creams on the beach, about this or that book she has just finished.

Now that the birth is so close, Hazel has begun to feel more peaceful. Excited in a tentative, hopeful way. She has bought a set of cotton chemises for him, a supply of napkins, a little wool cap, and put everything in the bottom drawer of the chest in her own bedroom. He will be born here at home. She pictures Grace propped up against the pillows, her proud smile, her white finger gripped in his new fist. Everything behind them, the mess she and Sylvia have made. Each thing—the move to the new house, the buying one by one of his miniature garments—has felt like a small repair to their lives.

Only sometimes, there's a cold fluttering in Hazel's throat, a falling in her stomach as if she's descending too fast in the shaft of a lift. She's afraid that there's something in all of this that is not quite as it should be, that their situation, on the brink of the baby's arrival, should be in some way different.

Sometimes, in the evenings, when Grace is upstairs sleeping, and she and Sylvia are together in the front room—Sylvia reading in her chair under the lamp in the corner, while she knits by the window—Hazel feels the press of their silence in the little rented room, looks across it at her sister and asks herself if there isn't something in all her careful preparations that she has failed to take care of. It preys on her, the fear that she's missed something, that she's left something out.

She wonders if Sylvia looks at herself sometimes, as she has, in the mirror, and asks herself if she could have made things turn out differently by being, perhaps, just a little more beautiful.

'Penny for them', she whispers softly to her sister one night near the end. But Sylvia doesn't even look up from her book, perhaps she doesn't hear, and the silence about it all that they've grown so used to glides over them again, still and heavy like water.

She watches Sylvia in the mornings when Grace comes down in her nightie for breakfast. She watches her sister's crumpled face searching for another spot in the little kitchen to rest her eyes, to save herself the agony of having to look at her daughter.

Hazel wonders how, exactly, the stranger's visit replays itself in her sister's mind, how exactly Sylvia feels about what has happened.

Sylvia looks these days, like a woman in mourning. Her mouth, unpainted, sags at the corners. She dresses in long cardigans and shapeless skirts, in thick stockings and flat-heeled shoes, but then, doesn't Hazel do more or less the same? Doesn't she have a horror of the way the two of them used to rig themselves out? The black slacks, the soft inviting sweaters? Don't the two of them look the same now, a pair of sad repentant twins? Two middle-aged women, a stoop beginning in their narrow cardiganed shoulders because of the weight they both carry, the weight of the guilt and the shame?

But Hazel can't say for sure what goes on in her sister's mind as she sits there in her chair on the other side of the silent room, because they've never talked about it to each other, never talked about any of it except that once when it became clear what the man had done. Like Grace's post-cards, their talk is always of ordinary things, of anything but what's happened. It's about the quality of Sunday's pork shoulder, about the new shape of the dunes after last night's winds. Like Grace, they've stayed silent, mute, about the other thing, about the stranger and the baby who'll be with them soon.

Every evening now, before the light goes completely, Hazel knits by the window of the plain rented room. The blanket is nearly finished, there's just the border to do now. Knit one, slip one, a different rhythm from the rest.

Tonight Grace has come to sit with her aunt. Sylvia has gone to bed early. She said she felt tired. Hazel knits. From time to time she looks up so she can smile at Grace. Looking at her after looking at Sylvia is like a balm, her clear skin, her steady mouth. She looks peaceful, contented, very, very young. Hazel feels herself soften, relax, the fearful flutter in her throat subsides. However painful this has all been for them, whatever the horrible confusion is that torments Sylvia, Grace is here, Grace is safe.

Hazel knits with smooth and incredible speed. She tells Grace she'll have the blanket finished in another couple of evenings.

Grace sits for a while watching her aunt's fast hands. Her breath, Hazel notices, has begun to grow shorter, more difficult these past few days with the full weight of him inside her.

Grace reaches out and strokes the soft blue wool. Hazel smiles back at her, hoping that her smile will say that everything will be all right, that the blanket will be given to the baby when he is born in another week or so and that it will keep him safe and warm.

Then Grace asks, 'Who is the blanket for?'

Hazel stops knitting, lays her work down in her lap. A chill settles beneath her heart and the room seems to shrink around her, seems to press in on her with the full force of the silence they have preserved so carefully, she and Sylvia, wanting only to put their crime behind them, wanting only—surely—to protect Grace, to make things easier for her, to do the best they can.

Who is the blanket for?

The girl's question hangs between them by a hair.

'For the baby, love,' says Hazel quietly, leaning forward and taking Grace's hand.

Grace blinks, tilts her head.

'What baby?'

Acknowledgements

The author would like to thank the editors of the following publications where some of these stories first appeared:

The 2007 Fish Prize Anthology: 'Waking the Princess'
The 2005 Bridport Prize: 'Rose Red'
Don't Know A Good Thing (the Asham Award short story collection, Bloomsbury): 'Hwang'.
The London Magazine: 'Historia Calamitatum Mearum'
Kestrel: a shorter version, under a different title, of 'Pied Piper'

Stories in this collection have won or been shortlisted for several awards, including: 'Monday Diary' won second prize in the 2002 Orange/Harpers&Queen Short Story Competition; 'Rose Red' was a runner-up in the 2005 Bridport Prize; 'Hwang' won second prize in the 2005 Asham Award; 'The Visitors' was shortlisted in the 2005 Fish Short Histories Prize; 'Waking the Princess' was a runner-up in the 2006 Fish Short Histories Prize; and 'In Skokie' was shortlisted for the 2006 Fish One Page Story Prize.

Extracts from *Latin For Even More Occasions* in 'Historia Calamitatum Mearum', reprinted by permission of HarperCollins Publishers Ltd © Henry Beard, 1991.